P9-AQN-270

DATE DUE

'83

A Ceremony

in the

Lincoln Tunnel

# BOOKS BY RICHARD CUNNINGHAM

THE PLACE WHERE THE WORLD ENDS

A CEREMONY IN THE LINCOLN TUNNEL

*Any resemblance between the characters herein (and I include the Lincoln Tunnel and the Hudson River under this genus) and actual persons living or dead is purely coincidental.*

Richard Cunningham

# A
# Ceremony
# in the
# Lincoln Tunnel

SHEED ANDREWS AND McMEEL, INC.
Subsidiary of Universal Press Syndicate
KANSAS CITY

**Library of Congress Cataloging in Publication Data**

Cunningham, Richard, 1939-
    A ceremony in the Lincoln Tunnel.

    I. Title.
PZ4.C97315Ce [PS3553.U495] 813'.5'4    78-14995
ISBN 0-8362-6105-4

*For*

Lucia and Shannon and Pablo

In partial payment for aid

and comfort beyond the

call of duty during

the long Valley Forge

of this second

book.

And thus I came to understand that I, anyhow, had had plague through all those long years in which, paradoxically enough, I'd believed with all my soul that I was fighting it. I learned that I had had an indirect hand in the deaths of thousands of people; that I'd even brought about their deaths by approving of acts and principles which could only end that way. Others did not seem embarrassed by such thoughts, or anyhow never voiced them of their own accord. But I was different; what I'd come to know stuck in my gorge. I was with them and yet I was alone. When I spoke of these matters they told me not to be so squeamish; I should remember what great issues were at stake. And they advanced arguments, often quite impressive ones, to make me swallow what nonetheless I couldn't bring myself to stomach. I replied that the most eminent of the plague-stricken, the men who wear red robes, also have excellent arguments to justify what they do, and once I admitted the arguments of necessity and *force majeure* put forward by the less eminent, I couldn't reject those of the eminent. To which they retorted that the surest way of playing the game of the red robes was to leave to them the monopoly of the death penalty. My reply to this was that if you gave in once, there was no reason for not continuing to give in. It seems to me that history has borne me out; today there's a sort of competition who will kill the most. They're all mad over murder and they couldn't stop killing men even if they wanted to.

Albert Camus   —   *The Plague*

I would like to thank The Port Authority of New York and New Jersey for its assistance. My gratitude goes also to:

Albert Bernal          (Ancient Mariner)

Charles Webb          (Scuba Buff)

Tim R. Menton          (Electronics Wizard)

Frederick Reines          (Genial Physicist)

W. Conger Beasley, Jr.          (Editor *Par Excellence*)

James Andrews          (Patient Publisher)

# Hogtalk

# One

~~

*(October 18th; 9:30 A.M.)*

"It takes about ninety seconds," the old hog said.

*

You go down the Jersey ramp and pause at a line of toll booths before plunging into the wide horseshoe portal, failing for the nth time to notice how quickly the passage shrinks, tapering off like a speaker on an old victrola while you pick up speed, leaving the morning behind on a gentle curve that drops suddenly into the tunnel's throat: a deadlevel corridor of palewhite tile bathed in yellow light by fluorescent lamps strung high like piping along one side, the concave walls causing sound to spiral so that air whooshes and tires whine high-pitched as birth or rumble like some wounded subterranean thing, and by then it is damp and the rectangular ceiling grates are widest because you've gone under the Hudson, lying a few scant feet above your head while a series of images stream by like accelerated movie film: little gray doors in the walls and overhead traffic lights (three horizontal eyes blinking in the end of what looks like a converted muffler) and oddlooking cylinders bolted near the roof and a glassed-in metal booth where a policeman sits and a tiny vehicle resembling a motorcycle sidecar standing by the

1

~~

catwalk rail—a montage as brief and mysterious as the faces on a crowded street, looming up and slipping past until all at once the roadway tilts and the tube begins telescoping outward and behind you a semi downshifts with an incredible roar, the big gears straining, pulling as you are pulling for the shaft of light spilling around the final looping bend that shoots you out into Manhattan, where it is morning again.

\*

"That's ninety seconds one way," a second, even older hog said in a reedy voice. "Three minutes round trip."

"Jesus," said the first hog, "don't reveal your education, Salvador." He turned back to the reporter. "Like I was sayin, ninety seconds. That ain't no trip; it's a stampede. Four years and eight men dead in the doin, and you can whiz through it in about the time it takes to piss off a load of beer. Hell, mister, in 1934 it took ninety days just to decide where to *put* the damn thing."

\*

It took hydraulics and geology and geophysics: topographic surveys and borings for core samples in the riverbed; stratigraphic maps outlining rock formations; charts on tide, current, depth—a mass of data tunnel engineers sifted for weeks to determine size and length and gradient. Then estimates: cement, steel, cast-iron, lumber, pipe, labor, gasoline, electricity, even light bulbs. Next architectural plans for access roads, approaches, ventilation towers, an administration building. Then money, most of it New Deal. Finally they let the contracts; ground was bought and cleared.

\*

"Them was hard times, you know," the first hog said. "Durin the Depression. Long before your day."

"It was the post-Depression, Gunny," Salvador said. "The crash come in twenty-nine."

Gunny shrugged. "We got a historian here."

"There was a bootleg war on," Salvador continued. "I remember, because it was about the time they discovered that giant in Persia."

"How'd we get to *Persia*?" Gunny asked. "Will you listen to this? Salvador, the man don't require a course in geography. He's writin about the Lincoln."

"Ten foot six inches tall, he was," Salvador insisted, his voice beginning to squeak as it rose. "Can you feature the jock *he* must've had?"

\*

Ironworkers assembled the caisson—a huge watertight steel box open at the top but furnished with an airtight bulkhead eight feet above the botton, which had a cutting edge. Once finished, fire tugs towed the caisson upriver on its side where engineers upended it in shallow water just off the New York shore. They pumped the water out of the cavity above the bulkhead, then cleared the compartment beneath with compressed air so that workmen could go through the air lock and begin excavating soil, which was sent through a material lock and hauled topside for dumping. When enough earth had been removed, they poured concrete into the caisson's hollow sides to force the cutting edge down, whereupon the workers went through the airlock once more and resumed digging. In this manner the caisson was driven to grade. The tunnel eventually passed through the lower chamber (providing an alignment check), and afterwards the caisson functioned as an escape valve in case of disaster.

Workmen under the bulkhead toiled knee-deep in slime, using spades and mattocks to dislodge the clay and muck, which coated them by the end of their shift, when they emerged looking like coal miners and smelling like fermented sileage, which explains why they were called sandhogs, a term generic to New York and abridged, among themselves, to hog.

\*

"The bottom?" Gunny said. "Sand and silt for a few feet, then clay—the Hudson goop. Black and thick, sticky . . . kind've like fudge in a way. The work compartment was cramped and smelly, and air pressure blew water and mud all over—in your mouth and hair, in your eyes, up your *ass*hole when you bent over. Water was always seepin in, but we only had a few small blowouts. . . . Blowout? Well, compressed air, see, works on the same principle as a straw. I mean, when you blow on a straw you force the water out, right? And it stays out as long as you keep on blowin. It's the same in tunnel work, only the pressure has to be strong enough to hold back the river and the mud. A blowout is when air escapes through a pocket in the mud. You lose pressure and the mud caves in. Lots of hogs drowned in blowouts in the old days. But we didn't have none that was serious. All the same, it was a bitch under that caisson, with the heat and the mud and the stink. Wasn't nothin good about it."

"I didn't work on the caisson," Salvador explained.

"That was the only good part," said Gunny.

*

Mechanics installed giant air compressors on both sides of the river. Blasting crews began digging a seventy-foot shaft on each shore from which the two headings would proceed. Steam shovels, derricks appeared. Machinists set about forging thousands of steel points for the pneumatic drills. For some time a team of doctors had been examining job applicants, weeding out those with physical defects which barred them from working under compression. (No heart, lung, or ear problems. Sinus afflictees not welcome. No claustrophobiacs need apply.) After the shafts were completed, drillers and dynamiters hacked the tunnel through rock until they reached soft ground, then a shield was lowered in sections to the bottom of each shaft.

Visualize a squat, four-hundred ton, steel-plated whiskey tumbler eighteen feet long, thirty-one feet in diameter, lying on its side. That gives you a general idea of what the shield looked like. The thick sides tapered to a cutting edge at the "rim"—the top of which protruded four feet beyond the bottom to serve as a steel canopy protecting sandhogs excavating out front from cave-ins. The "bowl" or working face was made up of vertical and horizontal ribs, tiered working platforms, and trap doors that could be opened to admit earth. Twenty-eight hydraulic jacks, each with a thrust of two hundred tons, were bolted to the "bottom" or rear of the shield. Braced against cast-iron rings which formed the tunnel lining, the jacks propelled the cutting edge in a crunching thirty-two-inch shove, at which point they retracted and a huge erector arm attached to the rear of the shield set another ring in place—lifting each of the fourteen crescent-shaped sections and pivoting like the hands on a clock until the circle closed. They carted off most of the mud that oozed through the trap doors, spreading some beneath the walkway for ballast. Ring diameter was four inches smaller than the shield, so after bolting the sections together they hosed concrete grout into the space between earth and lining, and then all was ready for the next thirty-two-inch shove. Slowly, grinding away twenty-four hours a day, seven days a week, both shields began to core the riverbed.

*

"We didn't work regular hours, you know," Gunny said. "We did two three-hour shifts with a three-hour break in between. On account of the nitrogen build-up in your body."

"*Just six hours*," Salvador piped. "Three on, three off, then three on again."

Gunny glanced behind him. "There's an echo in here some-place." He gave Salvador a look before going on. "My shift begun at eight in the mornin, which meant we got to the hoghouse early . . . the hoghouse?"

"A big tin *shed*," Salvador broke in, "where you could get a bite to eat and bunk down between shifts."

"Right," said Gunny, staring at Salvador. "So as I was *sayin*, after a bit the shift foreman, which in this case was me, yelled it was time to go."

\*

By elevator down the shaft and into the tunnel, following narrow-gauge railroad tracks to a cylindrical air lock embedded high overhead in the concrete bulkhead. Up muddy wooden stairs to give their badges to the checker, who hung them on pegs and noted the time in his log. When the lock tender opened the door, they climbed in and sat on one of the two wooden benches, making small talk until the tender swung the door shut with a bang.

\*

"Some guys chew gum," Salvador said. "Swallowin helps, too. But the best thing is to hold your nose like this and blow."

\*

The first inrush of air rocked the cabin with a powerful hiss that gathered maddening intensity as the pressure increased. Pinching their nostrils shut, they cleared their eardrums constantly. The temperature climbed steadily, and beads of sweat broke out on their faces while the door windows misted over, and still the pressure rose, driving their heads down in the attitude of prayer until they seemed some strange peasantry at worship in a makeshift Turkish bath where the pipes had broken. Then all at once the roaring faded to a loud whine that waned, dying like a cry of despair, and the hand on the pressure gauge stopped moving. A few seconds later the tender opened the far door and, ears pinging, their bodies bearing four atmospheres of pressure, they climbed out.

\*

"You gotta cup your hands and shout into the other guy's ear in order to talk," Gunny said. "Because once you leave the lock it's like bein inside a tin can with somebody beatin on the outside with a stick. You couldn't hear a whale fart."

*

A string of light bulbs hung along one wall, dimly outlining a wooden walkway that ran beside the tracks, down which came laborers pushing small open cars filled with muck headed for the material lock. Bare tunnel rings coiled like internal threads on a screw toward the far end where the shield stood illuminated by big ceiling lamps. The boards underfoot were sloppy, the air muggy and foul-smelling. They passed under a platform ten feet above the floor on which three black men worked mixing grout, their faces gray with cement dust. By then, and for the next three hours, the surge of compressed air boomed against the walls like surf.

*

"Hey!" Salvador cried in his high-pitched voice. "I just thought of somethin for your article. You couldn't take a water-proof watch down there because the pressure would blow the crystal off."

About to swallow, Gunny took his lips from the bottle of beer. "In 1934 you had a *watch*?"

*

Sound waves slow at a depth of one hundred feet. In tunnel work all noise develops resonance, is distorted, and metal can groan like a cello lamenting Tristan's fate. Eight-pound bolts cry out when wrenched. Trap doors squawk open, closed with a loud dinng. The erector arm creaks lifting those seven-foot ring sections, which thud like a gong when they slam home. Hammers clang; a quartet of hydraulic bolt-tighteners brrrt-brrrt like drum rolls; pipes chime in. Things whistle and bang and bronnng and screak and bellow and wail in a rude and dissonant mix—a kind of Wagner gone metallic, the whooshing air his furious theme. At rare moments during a lull, the compressor's intake valve could be heard flapping like someone beating time with a cane.

*

"Once the shield's gone forward," Gunny said, "all you got between yourself and the river is about sixteen feet of mud. So you have to hustle. We used big hand ratchets, four-footers, on the bolts first, then a guy come behind with a hydraulic gun to finish the job. Even so, it took about ninety minutes to set the ring, bolt it, grout it in, and get ready for the next push. Meanwhile you gotta rely on the stand-up time of the clay, which under the Hudson is considerable. In most places. But a blowout can happen anytime, so you move fast. What? . . . Hell, I seen a hundred blowouts."

Salvador cut in with: "Everything gets *foggy*," his hand describing a half-moon arc in the air as though he were blessing the table. "Because pressure is leakin out and moisture is comin in. You can't hardly see the wall lights. Some guys panic, just drop everything and run. Because it's scary and the air is whistlin like a big teakettle and all the time it's gettin darker . . . What do you do?"

"You throw any shittin thing within reach into the *hole* is what you do," Gunny said. "Because it gets bigger all the time. Boards, benches, tools, cement bags . . . guys like Salvador. In the old days they kept bales of straw handy."

"Creegan was his name," Salvador said suddenly, looking at the ceiling. "Shot up like he was blowed from a cannon, he did." He brought his eyes back to the table. "Put *that* in your article," he urged the reporter, gesturing with the bottle. "Nineteen-o-five. On the old Rapid Transit tube under the East River. There was this guy Creegan who got caught in a blowout. He was tryin to plug it with a bale of hay and got sucked right up in the mud with only his legs hangin down. Then he just squirted out of sight. The air pressure slung him up through the mud and water, and he come to the surface on a spout as big as Old Faithful. Some longshoremen rescued him. Same thing happened in nineteen-sixteen to a hog named William Mabey. Blowed clear out of the Hudson. Lived, too. There was another fellow come up with him but he hit a boat and died. I'll just go get us another round."

Gunny smiled at the reporter's question. "No, he's tellin the truth. He can't remember to zip his fly half the time, but old Salvador's a bona fide elephant on dates and names. Spends half his time in the public library reading room. That really happened to them fellows. Hell of a ride, huh? . . . No, we didn't have nobody die in blowouts on the Lincoln. They died in other ways."

Salvador came back with the beer. "You see the chest on that lady bartender?" he asked, sitting down. "My God what tits."

Gunny ignored him. "How? Well, the first two died when a freak gas pocket exploded while they was out front of the shield. You can generally tell a gas pocket by the hollow sound it makes when a pick strikes it. When you hit one, you bore a hole in the mud and get down flat and then light the gas as it comes out. Makes a flame like a blowtorch. Them guys, though, they hit a *big* pocket. Went off like a bomb."

"Boy, five minutes," Salvador said dreamily. "I'd just like five minutes with her."

"You couldn't get five minutes out of your cock if you soaked it in a deep-freeze overnight," Gunny told him. "The others? Dynamite. All five died in the same explosion. It was freakish, too. We'd struck rock close to the New York side and had to blast it out of the way. So first the drillers highballed holes in the rock and then planted dynamite sticks with timed fuses. We hauled the debris off after the explosion so they could move back in to sink another cluster of holes. What happened was this big Chink driller hit a stick of dynamite that hadn't gone off before. It must've still been buried in the rock was the best anybody could figure. Blew both his arms off. Killed four Americans besides." Gunny paused and took a long pull on the bottle. "You know, in some ways goin *back* through the lock was the worst part of the whole day."

*

Decompression. A man working under the weight of several atmospheres cannot exhale all the nitrogen he breathes in; some instead is carried by the blood into body tissue—much in the same way carbon dioxide is forced into soft drinks. So long as decompression occurs slowly, the nitrogen exits as innocently as it entered. But if pressure is lowered too fast, the gas forms a froth of bubbles which tend to concentrate at bone joints, causing pain that even in a mild attack is excruciating. In severe cases the bubbles can clog the veins entirely, bringing instant death from heart embolism.

Which meant the hogs spent nearly an hour in decompression at the end of each shift: waiting while the tender periodically turned a valve and air swished out, mist forming once more on the windows, obscuring the cabin, which suddenly grew cold and dank as a cellar in fall, the air rustling like a flurry of leaves while they sat shivering and rubbing their goose bumps and staring aimlessly at the floor.

*

"The bends?" Gunny scoffed. "Hell, every hog on earth's had the bends. You can't expect to work in tunnels and not get them once in a while. Most guys would sweat them out at home; you didn't get no pay in the hospital."

Salvador raised his arm. "See that? Some morning it's twisted back like a grasshopper's leg. Permanent arthritis from hoggin. Started in my wrist and walked right up my elbow. Doctor says it's still creepin."

"I'm wonderin will I live to see it get to your mouth," Gunny said. "We're discussin the bends, not old age."

*

Caisson disease. Alternately referred to as the "bends," the "staggers," or the "screws." May strike hours, sometimes days after decompression. Frequently confused with drunkenness. General symptoms: a slight sensation of heat in the early stages, often followed by prolonged itching and rising temperature until . . .

. . . until you are on fire sitting up in bed and all the objects in the room are going blur, and then the dizziness and stuttering and pissing the bed before it really hits—a sudden lancing pain in the chest and then the pincers lunging from shoulder to elbow to calf as you fight for air, clawing at the sheets and crying out in a hoarse animal voice as it drags you by the scrotum to that dark whirling place where the agony comes wave after wave after wave until you are drowning in pain, doubled over in convulsions and choking on the puke and wanting to die before it breaks, leaving you limp and retching on the pillow, the wife holding your head and crying in a frightened voice: "Honey, God Honey is it over? odearGod Honey . . ."

\*

"In the old days, guys wore bracelets of zinc and silver to ward off the bends," Salvador said.

"The eighth death?" Gunny said. "That was Benny Reagan. Only he didn't get killed in the tunnel. He died in a police station in the Bronx."

Salvador looked down. "Poor little Benny."

"Sure I knew him," Gunny said. "Everybody knew Benny. He was hoggin on my crew the day he died. . . . It was a payday, so we stopped off for a few quick ones on the way home, Benny and me, because we was both livin in the Bronx then. I left him about an hour later, standin by the piano singin one of them Irish songs."

"He had a nice high voice," Salvador recalled. "Good as Dennis Day's. And he could've been a star except he was lame in one foot and walked funny."

"He wasn't no cripple, understand; he just didn't walk right," Gunny said. "And *fight*—Christ, he'd swing on a nun when he was loaded. So like I said, I left. Around nine his wife called me. Said Benny hadn't showed up yet. She was worried, so I told her I'd go round him up. He wasn't in the bar where I left him, though. They'd kicked him out, the third time that month, for startin a fight. I spent a half-hour duckin into bars before I come to a Greek dive near Fordham. The Greeks remembered Benny, all right. He'd busted a chair over some guy and dumped a spittoon on one of the waiters. They was all jabberin to themselves in Greek about it, wantin to know if I'd pay for the lousy chair, and that's when the whore come up and give me Benny's badge—the one all hogs wear on their shirts, that identifies a guy as a compressed air worker and says if he's sick you should take him to the Port Authority Lock.''

"Somethin like what them epileptics wear around their neck,'' Salvador added.

"She told me Benny had been actin funny when he come in, stutterin and fallin down, and the fight started when the Greeks tried to throw him out. Said the waiter had took his badge after three of them stomped the shit out of him, and threw it in a corner before they rolled him outside. Said he laid out there shakin all over and couldn't talk when the cops arrived. Said the Greeks told the law he was a wino. It took me thirty minutes to get to the station.

"After I explained about Benny, the desk-sergeant told another cop to get an ambulance ready. Then he took me back to the drunk tank. See, they tossed him in there thinkin he was a wino, so they didn't pay no attention to his screamin and kickin because they figured he had the crazies. Wasn't nobody else in the tank that early, and Benny was layin wedged under a bunk with one arm caught in the springs, and of course he was dead. The Greeks claimed the waiter didn't take his badge, and we couldn't find the whore, and who'd've believed her anyway? The cops didn't want no publicity, either. So nothin happened. That was forty years ago, but you know I can still remember what he looked like, his face all twisted up and his mouth wide open, like he was singin . . . I'll buy this time.''

After a bit Salvador said: "It took us a year to hole through—that's when the two headings connect up. And they was only a quarter-inch out of alignment. Not bad, huh? Of course, they didn't open it for another two and a half years.''

*

They cleaned out the silt and caulked the joints and poured a fourteen-inch concrete lining around the inside. They laid the plumbing and built the roadway (twenty thousand cubic yards of concrete) and strung sixty thousand miles of wiring. Year one.

One million four-inch-square ceramic tiles went into the ceiling. They put up the walls with one and one-half million glazed-tile blocks. By then the ventilation towers (one of which stood on the site where the caisson had been sunk) were nearly finished. Electricians moved in to install the lighting. Year two.

Stone masons set the last coping on the administration building two months before the paint dried on traffic lanes on the access roads and approaches. Signs went up about the time glaziers walked away from the toll booths. And then one day, after three years and eight months, it was done.

*

"The opening ceremony was impressive," Gunny said. "Babe Ruth was a guest speaker. Old Babe himself."

"Some nut waited in line over thirty hours to be number one in drivin across," Salvador said. "He's famous now for bein first at all kinds of events, but the Lincoln was where he got his start. And two crazy sonsabitches tried to ride through on horses just before they cut the ribbon, but the cops chased them out. Had to hold things up while a patrolman scooped the plop off the roadway."

"Then the Babe got in a car with the mayor and made the first trip," Gunny said proudly.

"It took about ninety seconds," said Salvador.

*

. . . down the ramp into the wide horseshoe portal, leaving the morning behind on a gentle curve that dropped suddenly into the tunnel's throat, a deadlevel corridor of palewhite tile bathed in yellow light by fluorescent lamps strung high like piping along one side, the concave walls causing sound to spiral so that air whooshed and tires whined high-pitched as birth or rumbled like some wounded subterranean thing . . .

# Two

~~~

A small crowd, mostly prostitutes (it was 2:40 A.M.; Paris, August 2nd), had gathered in a semicircle around the body (over which a police photographer crouched, impassive as a bird of prey) by the time Detective Rousseau arrived. As he stepped from the car, a short bowlegged gendarme ran up to him.

"He's a mess, sir. We're still trying to find half of him."

Rousseau nodded. He'd seen dismemberments. (Although disintegration was perhaps a more accurate term—the man had fallen two hundred and thirty-eight feet to the pavement, literally exploding on impact.) "Has anyone made an identification?"

The gendarme pointed to a building towering behind the crowd. "The concierge. His name was Rene Boule, age forty-seven. He lived in a penthouse suite."

"Alone?"

"The place was empty when we got here. According to the concierge, he was married but separated from his wife."

"Any witnesses?"

"Not so far. I sent a man to check with the tenants."

Rousseau nodded again and crossed the street, giving the corpse a passing wincing glance before going up the walk, the little gendarme wobbling beside him like an obedient bulldog. He paused outside the foyer. "*Bien*, Sergeant. Locate as many of the

~~~

parts as possible. And get those . . . citizens . . . away from here.''

"Very good, sir.'' The gendarme craned his neck back and gazed at the building soaring into black sky. "Makes you wonder, eh? Why a guy living in a palace like this, making plenty of dough and hobnobbing with royalty, would take the dive.''

"What was he, a painter?''

The gendarme snapped his fingers. *"Merde*, I forgot to tell you. He was Baron Rothschild's personal pilot.''


The kitchen was L-shaped, roomy. Plants in pots encased by hemp webbing hung from ceiling hooks. Dark cabinets with square bronze knobs formed geometric patterns on cheery-green walls. The red tile floor gleamed. Gloved like a burglar, Rousseau examined a blender with a beige rubber cap and two rows of beige buttons. He pulled down the self-cleaning oven door and peered into its shiny interior. Hefting an electric coffee pot, he admired the array of big knives and cleavers sheathed in a wooden frame next to an ornate case with a glass face behind which spice bottles rose tier after tier. The refrigerator (an enormous green cube with two doors and a trunk-sized freezer) contained enough food to feed a man for a month. On a tray on a wooden butcher's block inlaid in a formica counter that ran the length of one side sat a drum-shaped aromatic cheese surrounded by sausages, peppers, onions, a log of pastrami, two half-loaves of bread, a cluster of lavender garlic bulbs. Rousseau leaned over, sniffed, sighed. He knelt beneath the sink and looked inside the dishwasher: glasses sparkled, silverware glowed, bright clean plates stood racked like records. A low basket bulged with fruit at the counter's end. He broke off a clump of grapes and followed an arched vestibule around to the bar.

Also well stocked: a wide panel of gaily-colored bottles and glasses of all description. Neatly arranged on a shelf, more expensive hardware: stirring spoons, assorted corkscrews, two round-bottomed blenders, paring knives, strainers, an hourglass-shaped shot measurer. Light fixtures lay mirrored in the bar-top's satiny finish. At the sink a lone martini shaker rested upside-down like a crystal fez.

Beyond the bar, a dining room: twelve high-backed mahogany chairs lining a long table covered with a rich lemon cloth on which a silver candelabrum centerpiece, resembling the forked end of a trident, was the only adornment. Overhead, a glittering chandelier encircled by a band of prisms dangling like tassels.

Beyond the dining room, a den: two book-coated walls; another filled with prints, a dart board, photographs. A pair of skis propped in one corner down from an open roll-top desk against a window overlooking the park (and now the body) below. Leafing through a stack of papers, Rousseau came upon a curious document: paid reservations for two made out to Rene Boule for ten days (beginning August 7th) at Caesars Palace Hotel in Las Vegas, Nevada. He pocketed the receipt, tossed the grape stem into a waste can and retraced his steps past the kitchen, heading across the entryway and into the other wing.

Along the hall to a dome-ceilinged bathroom: a glistening white cavern smelling of fresh pine, the slick tile floor composed of blue and gold hexagons. Heavy blue towels with a velvety nap folded on golden rods. Spotless mirrors: one full-length beside a bureau, another over the faucets, a third mounted on the medicine chest—which bordered on a miniature pharmacy. Alongside the sunken marble bath, a bidet with narrow porcelain footpads and a spout sticking up like a conical ivory phallus. The shower stall was damp, still beaded in places, the soap moist. On his way out, Rousseau lifted the toilet lid, exposing a snowy bowl that sloped into a blue, pine-scented pool. Unzipping, he fumbled for himself, braced one gloved hand against the wall and urinated noisily, watching the amber bubbles rise.

Excepting the rumpled king-sized bed (on which four paired monarchs could have conjugated freely), M. Boule's private chamber was orderly. At one end almond-colored drapes (partially drawn, admitting moonlight) fell in pleated folds onto the claret carpet. A matching walnut chest of drawers and dresser adjoined the far wall. Between them, a wicker hamper that held one set of sheets, a handful of garments. (Inspecting the contents, Rousseau pulled out a white shirt, noting with chagrin that it was cleaner and less wrinkled than the one he wore.) Two belamped night tables flanked the bed, on one a digital-clock radio, an ashtray fashioned from a block of lapis lazuli in which two lipsticked Gaulois cigarettes lay stubbed. Turning down the covers, the detective stared thoughtfully at the bottom sheet: a light-blue surface discolored by three grayish blots of dried semen: two middle-high, spaced several feet apart; one low and near an edge. A few moments later he stepped on a maroon button caught in the carpet, its tiny loop intact, the knot still kinked in a tight ball. Fingering it, he returned to the hall.

The entryway widened into a railed landing overlooking the sunken living room: immense, harmonious as open house. A grand piano in a nook beside the central stairway which tumbled into tawny carpet (so thick and flexible that Rousseau had the fleeting sensation of browsing on an artificial, woven beach) whose sweeping contours gave way to polished terrazzo at the half-open sliding doors leading onto the balcony.

Where it was cool, a soft breeze whispering reprieve before the advent of another boiling summer day. The great city, her lights shimmering like stars, spread out before him in all directions. Traffic streamed along the far-off boulevards in red and yellow lines: bending, crisscrossing, interlacing to spin Gothic designs on the darkened loom of morning, converging into distant neon beams which made one think of tubular glass being blown rather than people flowing through the arteries of Paris (rushing toward work or home, the refuge of prayer, some fierce reunion of the flesh—making for the untold harbors of their own desperate invention at that grim hour when the voyage is its loneliest); made one realize that, barring interference from ship propellers, a whale's death-cry can be heard by others of its kind two thousand miles away, while down there, in that turbulent, electric sea, the screams of a falling man would scarce have caused a ripple . . . made one think—

Of neatness. No mystery there: Boule had, of course, employed a maid; moreover, pilots were more particular than most men about cleanliness and order—a behavioral spinoff resulting from the metier, the constant demands of precision and painstaking attention to detail creating (since the price for carelessness was death) a permanent attitude. No puzzle his sensualism, either: those who live in close proximity to danger are prone to squeezing pleasure from life, their grip varying in degree depending on distance, and hence Boule, a civilized man who gambled his mortality in air-conditioned comfort, had indulged himself in a moderate manner—celebrating food, clothes, spirits, and fornication (but surely nothing *outre* here, those being in a sense, adding the cinema and God, the national pastimes); thus a day ago, maybe last night, he had unburdened his loins repeatedly (departing from the way of Epicurus, but an understandable gluttony, armed with a bachelor's rechargeable balls) into someone, probably a recent acquaintance (to wit that change of sheets), more than likely young and desirable, perhaps one of those stewardesses, for whom any man, especially middle-aged, could supply a rabid ardor. The hotel reservations could be explained in any number of ways. Assuming it was his, the button, obviously torn away with some violence, might easily have been an accident. And many suicides neglect to leave a note . . .

A barge groaned suddenly on the nearby Seine, jogging Rousseau from his reverie with its low marine lament. Looking down, he saw an ambulance pull in beside the body.

On leaving, he slid the doors shut and, in the act of turning, noticed something embedded in the metal moulding, stuck fast approximately two feet above the floor. He stooped and found himself regarding a fingernail: nearly whole, specks of blood and tissue clinging to the base, unpainted, square, almost certainly a man's.

Descending by elevator to the street, Rousseau discovered that Rene Boule's pajama shirt lacked a maroon button, that the smashed fingers on his left hand still retained their nails, and that the right hand had broken off and was missing.

"Dogs," the Sergeant said. "They run in packs along the river. Unless it landed near a sewer drain." The idea made him grimace. "In which case, rats."

In any case, they never found it.

# Three

~~~

*(October 18th; 11:24 A.M.)*

"Finest natural port in the world," Gunny said to the reporter as they sat eating sandwiches on a pier near Forty-sixth Street. "Biggest, too." He adjusted the drag on his reel, then pointed a ham-on-rye in the general direction of Staten Island. "Thirty thousand ships a year drop anchor out there. Second only to Rotterdam."

Salvador, bent over baiting his hook, wearing a baseball cap backwards like a catcher, said confidentially, "That's in Holland. Samuel Cunard, a tight-assed Nova Scotian by birth, he's responsible." He paused to cast.

"Do go on," said Gunny with his mouth full.

"See them barges aground on the Jersey side, mister? Antiques. Been around since the Civil War. Some go back far as the Erie Canal. A few of the piers, too. Just fallin apart, like the rest of Jersey. Big chunks rot off and float out in the harbor, form a regular log jam in the upper bay north of the Narrows. Corps of Engineers has to clean the river every day so's a piece of timber don't wreck some ocean liner's propeller. They collect the junk with the Driftmaster, startin from Gravesend Bay in Brooklyn every mornin. . . . The Driftmaster? It's kind've like a carpet sweeper—just a big hull ridin on twin pontoons like a catamaran,

20

~~~

with an open bow where the net hangs to catch debris. They pick up the damnedest things, you know. Pianos they've hauled in. Enough rubbers to build a Goodyear blimp. Horses, whales. And people, lots of them. Not the guys in cement shoes; that's East River. Not many babies, either; they get chucked down incinerators. Mostly suicides. Eels get to the bodies bad. Once they even snagged a dead giraffe out by the Statue of Liberty. Nobody *ever* figured out how it got there.''

''Wandered off from Little Africa,'' Gunny said, sticking a boiled egg at New Jersey. ''You think I'm jokin. Listen, once you leave the tunnel over there, buddy, you're in Nigeria, in the jungle—one continuous Frank Buck movie with ten million fuckin bearers comin outa the bush. They should re-name Newark Razorville. If they shook down every nigger in Newark, General Motors wouldn't have to buy *steel* for a year. Over there a kid gets a tiny little razor before he can walk. When he grows out of it, his folks bronze it alongside his baby shoes. The planet of the apes, that's Jersey. Mr. Giraffe was trying to swim to Africa, where there ain't so many niggers.'' He turned to Salvador. ''When do we hear from Cunard?''

''Ain't no need to talk about black people that way,'' Salvador said under his breath. ''You're lookin at a chamber pot, mister. Manhattan alone pumps two hundred and fifty million gallons of raw sewage a day into the river. Gives you some idea why the water is brown, don't it? . . . Sure, most of it washes out to sea. Eventually. But you gotta understand the currents. Bein a tidal river, the Hudson has reversin ocean currents: flowin south at flood, runnin north at ebb. Strong currents, too. Must reach five, six knots when the tide is goin out. But the river begins in the Adirondacks, up high, and it runs down north, a real mountain rapids at first, pickin up the Hoosic and Mohawk tributaries and growin wider, slowin down around Albany where the bed begins to level out, and it's near dead level for over a hundred miles before it merges with the ocean current. So there's two different currents on the river, playing tug-of-war in a way, which means you can drop a log in the water at Troy and it'd take two months to reach Manhattan.

"So, most of the shit washes away, but some of it settles and some of it stays, goin back and forth and gettin thicker, like stew, every year. Take my advice, don't stand near no ferry rail on a windy day, because the spray comes straight from the crappers of New York."

Gunny whispered furiously, "I got a *bite*! There's somethin on my *line*!"

"Funny thing is, the river don't die. Not down here. It's dead up above in some places, but down here the ocean keeps it alive. That water may be half bowel movement, but it's also one-quarter salt. The salt-line stretches over sixty miles; ocean fish use it like a tunnel to work their way upstream. Once there was sturgeon as far up as Port Edward. Hard to believe now. Me and Gunny been fishin the Hudson goin on forty years, and there ain't nothin quite like it. There's sea sturgeon, striped bass, carp (so big you need a Louisville Slugger to land them), white perch, shad, even mullet. Hell, sea anemones nest beneath the George Washington Bridge. Crab, lobster, bluefish, herring . . ."

". . . Come on, you son of a *bitch*, swallow it! Eat hearty on that cornmeal and caro! *Gag*, you cocksucker, *gag*!"

"Pollution don't seem to affect the fish. In fact, some of the best fishin was in the sewer at One Hundred Seventy-second Street and Riverside Drive years ago. They called it the Medical Center because there's a hospital nearby. The gunk pourin from the pipe was milky-white; formed a chalk-colored slick an inch thick on the surface. Looked like a layer of milk of magnesia. On cool days it'd steam, give off a smell would turn back a goat. . . . Why'd I fish there? It was a great place for bass. Evidently they thrived on milk of magnesia. I only quit because I couldn't stomach the crud you had to pick off the line after each cast."

"*Shit*fire!" Gunny cried in disgust. "You see what that bastard done?" He stood as the cruiser hummed by, thirty yards away, long and sleek and powerful. The man on the bridge waved.

"That's the third time this mornin he's come past. Awhile ago he was trollin on the Jersey side." He shook his fist at the boat, but the man at the helm had turned away, intent on his gauges. Reeling in, Gunny shook his head. "Scared a giant carp right off my hook."

Salvador made a face. "Carp. They got their start on the Hudson, you know. Henry Robinson of Newburgh, New York. He's the moron carted them back from Europe in 1831. Dumped them out upstream. They multiplied like weeds and the fishermen was crazy about them until they uprooted the wild rice and celery and drove off the ducks, churnin the bottom up so game fish couldn't see to hunt or hatch their eggs, and pretty soon the river was choked with them.

"Scientists tried every poison in the book and come to the conclusion nothin kills a carp. They're even tryin to get rid of them I heard with that LSD—makes them swim backwards in a stupor. The Jews used to make gefilte fish from Hudson carp till they got too oily. Now the gefilte comes from Kansas and Nebraska. Ain't many Jews out there, I guess."

Gunny snickered. "Hell, no. You can't hock wheat."

"Well anyway, so far the carp haven't turned on and tuned out. They're still oily, still multiplyin . . ."

". . . Like the coons in Jersey," Gunny added.

Salvador flashed Gunny an irritated look. "You got a lotta hate in you today." Then to the reporter he said: "The Fifty-ninth Street sewer was the best striped bass fishin in New York at one time. The water was warm year round, so we fished there mainly in the winter when the stink was down. Hell, executives used to drop by early in the mornin to fish an hour or so before work. We'd let blood worms down through a grate and if somebody hooked a bass they'd reel it up so everybody'd get a look, then cut it loose.

"Hey, remember when we fished the Seventy-second Street sewer?" Gunny asked. "That was *pure* sewage, man. You could count the *turds* as they rolled by. But durin a big striper run there'd be thirty people fishin from a walkway like they was standin on a pier. Mostly wops—uh, sorry Salvador, I mean Italians—fishin with drop lines, a few old-timers whalin away with sidewinder reels. We'd all be catchin bass like crazy. It was such a popular spot a game warden come by once in a while—you wasn't supposed to keep anything under sixteen inches long. The Italians beat that rap by choppin the head and tail off. You gettin cold?''

"A little,'' Salvador said testily without looking at him. "My favorite spot was the sanitation pier at One Hundred Thirtieth Street at night. When it was lit up and the tide was goin out, the fish'd come in swarms. I caught everything, includin the clap, at that pier. Me and Fishhead Simpson (he's a guy fished with me in those days) we seen a porpoise one evenin, just flyin along and jumpin, comin clean outa the water, playing. And once, on an early mornin, I seen a blackfish whale going up the Hudson, dark as ebony and shiny in the sunlight, swimmin in and outta patches of fog like a ghost, just him out there, makin a low kinda whistlin sound, all alone as if he owned the river. Most beautiful thing I ever seen in my life . . .''

Gunny started reeling in fast. "Come on, let's go back to the bar. I'm freezin my *nuts* off.''

As they were leaving, Salvador said, "There he is again.''

Far off, the cruiser slid along the Jersey bank, moving slowly against the current as if being towed by invisible men.

"Wonder what the hell he's doin,'' Salvador said, "goin up and down like that.''

\*

The *Vita-Vita,* a 1974 Matthews Sportfisher, was fifty-six feet long. Her British-built fiberglass hull measured sixteen feet across the beam. She was powered below deck by two 8-cylinder, 435-horsepower, turbocharged diesel engines mounted side by side just forward of the Duff-Norton sonar apparatus. Outlined against the river that afternoon, she had neither the streamlined grace nor the aesthetic appeal of a sailboat under way; but she was smooth and solid-looking from her flaring bow to the fighting chairs at her stern. Well-found and in perfect condition, the *Vita-Vita* could cruise at twenty knots.

Her cabin curtains were drawn. Inside, the salon was dank and gloomy. The furniture (two leather armchairs, a small couch, several end tables, the color TV and tapedeck) had been moved to starboard to make room for a pile of scuba gear (some of it still wet and muddy from the night before) strewn along the port wall.

There was a man sitting at the bar separating salon from galley, his gaze fixed on a cartoon in a Beirut newspaper printed three days earlier. The artist had drawn a caricature with two faces: the right half an outline of Jordan's Hussein, the left those well-known features of a Jew wearing an eye-patch. From force of habit, the man did not smile at the satire. On his ruined face the attempt would have been grotesque.

He was thirty-two years old, tall and powerfully built with an athlete's fluid proportions—a sense of motion gone skin deep, so that leaning over the paper he seemed nervous as a linebacker, coiled as if to spring. His hair was short, black like his eyes, which were flat and cruel. His left ear was missing, an ugly round crater in its place. Beginning under his left eye, his face was terribly disfigured by scar tissue, shiny and nearly transparent, spreading down his left cheek like a wrinkled contour map beneath which veins and arteries fanned out like tiny pulsating rivers flowing violet and red beneath the rose-colored surface that mutilated the nostril and then curved, taking half the mouth away (and leaving an opening of odd ridges and welts merged like melted plastic hardened into a permanent frown) before slanting across the neck and disappearing under the collar of his black turtleneck sweater.

Folding the paper, he rose suddenly, cat-like, and went below, climbing down a companionway ladder at the end of the bar. He walked to the end of the narrow corridor and entered the forward berth, a cramped triangular room with two double-bunk beds set at a 45-degree angle to one another. Both upper bunks were occupied. The two men slept fully clothed. Wrapped in canvas and tied down to the bunk supports, the body lay in the lower starboard berth. Bent bowlike from the constant rocking, it resembled a rolled-up hammock except for the bound feet sticking out and the blood-soaked area shrouding the head.

The scarred man flopped down on the empty lower berth. Closing his eyes, he listened to the engines growling in a low monotonous tone and felt the river sucking, heaving, whispering its own peculiar chant while he drifted toward sleep, sliding soon onto the back of a wave that bore him smoothly through darkness out of sound and time, its satiny crest falling, falling, lowering him into its silken lair, and he was not awake when the *Vita-Vita* lifted all at once, her engines leaping into full savage voice as she headed out toward the open sea for a private burial.

# Four

～

"I figure three guys," Rousseau said during a private conversation in the Prefect's office on August 10th. "Very capable professionals. Boule was a husky six-footer, in excellent shape according to his doctor, yet there are few signs of a struggle."

"Signs?" The Prefect smiled with his mouth shut, much like a professor listening to a dull student. "You mean that button?"

"Not exclusively. Several other clues turned up when I went over his bedroom with the maid later that morning. It seems she cleaned the place on August first while he was playing tennis. By her account, a lamp shade and its frame were newly dented. Also a credenza and an easy chair were slightly out of line—the carpet indentations bore this out. There were scuff marks on the wall where the bed had been banged around."

"Considering those volcanic orgasms you discussed in your report, I'm surprised it was still standing. Which reminds me—what about this girl?"

"Boule took her to lunch at the Coupole after tennis. He was well known there, and several people remembered her: she wore a green transparent blouse without a bra. Tall, very pretty, early twenties, long black hair, olive skin. The waiter who attended them has the impression, based on her accent, that she is a foreigner."

"But you can't find her?"

"No. However, I have three clean sets of prints . . ."

". . . Which, I understand, are not on file anywhere in France."

"True, but I don't think she's a French citizen . . ."

". . . Come now, you place too much stock in a waiter's fragmentary recollections."

"I don't know—waiters are attuned to foreign accents, especially in tourist spots like the Coupole."

The Prefect shifted his attention to the window, where a group of pigeons bobbed on the stone ledge. "Of course, she might just be another innocent girl with memorable breasts who was seduced by a handsome older man . . . engaged, say, to a young naval officer gone half the year at sea . . . made restless by the summer's heat, thighs aquiver, hormones smoldering . . . swept off her feet by a lusty stallion with the manners of a count . . . now understandably reluctant to come forward, hesitant to broadcast her promiscuity." He turned back to Rousseau with that smile again. "Who knows—the shock of such protracted ramming may have driven the poor girl into a convent."

Rousseau grinned like a man nursing a toothache. "She was a plant. I imagine she entered the country a few months ago on a temporary visa."

"You checked with all the foreign embassies? Immigration? Interpol?"

"Yes—nothing."

"*Quel dommage,*" the Prefect said pleasantly. "You know, Claude, I find it strange Boule never mentioned her to anyone."

"He was a very private man. Those who knew him say he didn't boast about his women."

"Ah," the Prefect understood, "a cavalier."

"A prudent cocksman," Rousseau corrected him. "A *bavard* would not have lasted long in Rothschild's confidential employ."

"I'm curious—how can you be certain it was *her* at the apartment?"

"We removed black pubic hair from the bed and the shower. The maid swears both were spotless when she left. None of his other girls have black hair. All of them, in fact, had solid alibis."

"How many others were there?"

"Three, on a steady basis. Two single, both brunettes; one blonde and married."

The Prefect raised his eyebrows. "Dear me, he *was* fit."

"So it was her. It looks like they'd been seeing each other for a month or so. A friend ran into them in Nice three weeks ago. Typically, Boule sent her into a shop and crossed the street alone to say hello. They'd become lovers, though my guess is not frequently. He was absent twice for several days ferrying Rothschild to Spain and Luxembourg. And he screwed both brunettes a couple of times—the blonde was on vacation with her family. None of *them*, by the way, received an invitation to Las Vegas."

"Why do you say she was a plant?"

"The latch was off. There are no signs of its having been forced."

"She left early. She's a nurse on the night shift. A telephone operator. A dancer in some discotheque."

Rousseau shook his head. "He would have seen her to the door, latched it behind her. Boule was too meticulous a man to neglect a thing like that. Besides, he had over two hundred thousand francs worth of sculpture and paintings in the living room, not to mention four thousand dollars in traveler's checks in his dresser—which incidentally rules out thieves. She may even have unlocked the door for them, although it jimmys easily with a stiff piece of clear plastic. Or they had a key. What's definite is that latch was off."

The Prefect rubbed one eye hard, digging the knuckles deep. "I see. Go on."

"Boule and the girl came back to the apartment at approximately four o'clock. He mixed a shaker of martinis, presumably before they went to bed. Later they ate a snack in the kitchen: the autopsy revealed undigested cheese, pastrami, and bread. It appears both showered after eating. I suspect the girl bathed first while Boule tidied up the bar and kitchen—it was his nature, and would have given her ample opportunity to rig the door when he was in the shower. Afterwards they returned to bed and she kept him there until he fell asleep.''

"Of utter exhaustion, one assumes," the Prefect said dryly.

"The killers entered around two in the morning. If he heard them at all, it was not until they were almost on him.''

The Prefect halted him with a raised hand. "Upon what is *that* uncanny observation based?''

"There was a pistol in one of the night tables. He would have gone for it.''

"Possibly he did but, worn out from manly exertions, lacked the power to hold it.''

"No. To open it, you have to push a button *beneath* the drawer edge which activates a spring-lock that only he and the maid knew about. There were no prints on it.''

"Then again, he may have been engaged in further drilling operations.''

"I doubt that; he landed with his pajamas on. In any event, there was a brief scuffle. Boule was no coward; he fought. But they were pros, experienced in beating people to death, so whatever happened happened fast. After they dragged him off, the girl dressed and straightened the bedroom.

"They got him onto the balcony before he broke loose. By then he must have known it wasn't robbery, must have sensed what was coming, and his panic gave him the strength to tear free. He made it into the living room before they caught him and clubbed him down, then started to pull him back through the doorway, so he grabbed it. We lifted his prints, all ten fingers, off the glass.

"He screamed twice—a neighbor one floor down claims she thought it was a dog howling. So they didn't waste much more time on him, wanting out of there quick and enraged by his refusal to die quietly: one guy on his feet trying to pry him loose while the others chopped and booted, aiming at the ribs, the arms, the neck—careful not to draw blood but unconcerned about the bones they broke; his hands slipping until he clung by just the fingertips, but still hanging on, stubborn, terrified, and then I figure all three grabbed him low and heaved, yanking so hard the nail ripped off, and he was airborne. They cleared out fast, forgetting or simply not bothering to erase his prints, which explains why they missed the nail.'' He thought for a few seconds. ''That's about what happened.''

''Fascinating,'' the Prefect said evenly. ''Colorful.'' He nodded to himself. ''I like it. Except for one minor detail you've omitted. What was the motive?''

Rousseau's face slumped. ''That's the problem—it just doesn't add up.''

''I quite agree. It subtracts.''

''Look, don't call off the investigation yet. Give me another week.''

''Impossible. We've kept the lid on this affair too long as it is. The Minister had an unpleasant meeting with reporters yesterday. They accused him of withholding information.''

''They were right.''

''Disclosing Boule's horizontal adventures would serve little purpose except to sell newspapers. More to the point, if we don't release a statement soon, the press will begin grinding out innuendoes. And we both know what that means.''

Rousseau gave a tired nod. ''It means the good Baron will be implicated, drawn by association into a pretty sordid mess. It means you're going to close the case to protect Rothschild's reputation.''

The Prefect looked at his watch. ''Good Lord, it's almost noon,'' he said cheerfully. ''Your time is about up.''

''You intend to call it suicide?''

''Of course not. Boule was a Catholic as well as a cocksman. In view of the ambiguity surrounding his death, and in the absence of any hard evidence indicating foul play, the Minister feels we have sufficient latitude to warrant exercising charity in order to spare his family. The ruling will be accidental death.''

''How does the Minister account for that fingernail?''

''He doesn't,'' the Prefect said calmly. ''And neither do you, seeing we have no hand to match it with.''

"The blood type corresponds with Boule's."

"Highly provocative; disturbing perhaps; but little more than circumstantial evidence from a legal point of view. And even if it *is* his—which frankly I take for granted—what does that prove, really? It could have been a freak accident, the pain inducing a mild case of shock that sent him stumbling across the balcony where, somehow, he fell."

Rousseau was astonished. "You can't believe that."

"Don't *tell* me what I believe," the Prefect snapped. "And don't waltz in here spouting theories based on a waiter's intuition and undigested cheese, expecting me to fall off my chair. I want *facts,* goddamit! Witnesses, prints, suspects, above all a motive—I want *evidence,* not a string of suppositions. Who the hell do you think you are, Inspector Maigret? Poring over pubic bristles as though they were tea leaves, tracking semen like some demented Apache—the next thing I know, you'll enlist a clairvoyant! If I took your argument to the Minister, he'd have us both directing traffic on the Boulevard Saint Michel!" He took a deep breath and went on in a lowered voice. "Now, since you can't produce the girl, the killers, or a motive, let alone one single fact to support a case for murder, to say nothing of an international conspiracy, I suggest you get your ass out of here before I lose my patience."

Rousseau stopped at the door. "If we arrest the girl?"

The Prefect smiled wearily. "Bring her to my office. Should her breasts live up to their fame, I'll speak to the Minister."

But they never found her, either.

# Five

~~

*(October 18th; 2:05 P.M.)*

Gunny glared at the reporter. "What the hell you mean, *'blow it up'*? Who'd try to blow up the tunnel?"

"Ain't no need to lose your temper," Salvador said in a beery voice. "He was only askin if it could be done. No law against that."

"Keep your nose in your beer, Salvador. Listen, mister—okay, say some loony fucker wanted to demolish the tunnel. I guess you never worked around dynamite, so you don't know when it explodes it follows the path of least resistance. Now: the walls are curved, and the tunnel is open in both directions east and west, which means the blast wouldn't have anything to brace against, which means you could line five semi-trailers loaded with *nitro* in the center of the tube and about all they'd do is shoot fire out both ends. They might blow down the wall and ceiling tile, but they'd never pierce the concrete, let alone the steel . . . Why not? Because of the Hudson. Which is sittin on top. Eighty feet of water. You got any idea how much weight that is per square foot? And below the Hudson is sixteen feet of mud. So in order to break a hole, you'd have to lift both of them outta the way. You know how much force it'd take to lift them just one inch?

33

~~

"Okay—say the same loon decides to blow it from the outside. For starters, he's gotta get to the bottom of the river and *find* the tunnel, right?"

"Absolutely," Salvador chirped. "No question about it."

"And the Hudson has some powerful currents, like Salvador said. Besides that, pilots say on the bottom the river swirls east, which means there's eddies down there could trap a diver so he couldn't get back *up*. All right, once he finds it, *if* he finds it (I mean, it ain't marked with neon lights, you know), he's gotta dig through sixteen feet of the thickest mud in the world. Which might take a little time. And time is his enemy, that deep. What's his air tank capacity, three hours? Okay—if he stays down that long he can't come up all at once or the nitrogen will kill him. He's gotta surface in stages, so many feet at a time, and meanwhile the current will be carryin him away.

"But for*get* all that shit, because I promise you he couldn't move enough mud in three hours to fill a good-sized barrel. Of course, he could swim down night after night and end up halfway to Holland every mornin, *if* nobody spotted him. But the Hudson ain't exactly empty of boats. There's also the harbor patrol. Roads on both sides; piers, too. Look, they got cameras mounted on buildings that rotate all around the approaches. Inside there's a string of television cameras to monitor traffic. And the Port Authority has cops at both ends and in the booths along the catwalk. With *guns*. So forget it, mister; there ain't no way to blow up the Lincoln."

"No way in the world," Salvador agreed, shaking his head. "Now, who's gonna buy the next round?"

# Splinter Group

# One

~~

"The Committee would like you to get a boat," was what George, his contact, had told him in August once they'd come downstairs after dinner for a drink in the Algonquin lobby. So officially it started there, in Arabic, over pale liqueurs in the sedate Algonquin, his favorite hotel.

Unofficially, however, it began nearly eighteen months earlier in 1973, in Beirut while he was on sabbatical—after dinner that time also, in Machiavelli's, his favorite restaurant (destroyed one month after the meeting by Israeli terrorists, killing three of his five former table companions while he was lecturing safely at NYU).

Began with a question from a man concerned (as were they all) by the outcome of recent events in Khartoum. The Organization's sources indicated that American military assistance to Israel had escalated alarmingly since the U.S. Ambassador's assassination. (The man drew a tedious cause-effect connection: enumerated shipments of A-4 Skyhawks and Phantom Jets, ground-to-air missiles; dwelt at length on a consignment of M-60 tanks equipped with computerized range-finders—rambling on and on as though in need himself of some aim-adjusting device.) Worse, Kissinger, of late grown even more devious in his efforts to circumnavigate the "Palestinian Problem," was reportedly arranging a *sub rosa* covenant between Sadat and Israel which involved reopening the

Suez Canal. (Kissinger at once amused, disturbed them. On one hand, a round little Jew shuttling back and forth like some latter-day Boswell, with Boswell's concern for appearances, that same allegiance to distinguished gab: a harmless courier warming his plump bottom at the hearth of greatness. And yet, beneath that bland and sonorous exterior lurked a Quiet American of the naturalized variety—ambidextrous as a Bedouin, bartering in blood, the world his stall). Moreover, his (Kissinger's, also by coincidence the Israelis') insistence upon Hussein as caretaker for the Palestinians was gathering considerable support in the U.S. Congress.

In view of these developments, further proof (if more indeed were necessary) of the American-Israeli conspiracy to exclude Palestine both diplomatically and in fact, the man suggested (strictly as contingency, mind you; a Rubicon in need of fording only if the river rose) a direct reprisal against the United States.

Could they not, for example, bomb one of those tunnels in New York?

Another man, an engineer at Exxon, thought any tunnel an absurd choice of targets.

So, for the hell of it, "But why?" he'd asked good-naturedly, his usual expansive Palestinian self: Abdul Nosser, teacher of physics, a big man with a bushy mustache and continental manners who exhibited the easy sympathies of a talk-show host; Abdul the professor, with his impeccable Cambridge doctorate, his U.S. Government research grants, the boy with the solid-gold cover who owned an apartment on Park Avenue, a place in Vail, a green Daimler, a Rodin, whose tailor numbered *two* Rockefellers among his clientele; Abdul of the brilliant mind and diverse accomplishments (who played a cello, sailed a boat), who seized ideas like bread, then broke them apart and chewed the pieces carefully— "Why *not* a tunnel?"

The engineer, a thin sour-looking Saudi (a pessimist, of late preoccupied with rumored Israeli designs on his life—and in this instance prescient: one of those blown to pieces a month later), said: "Too many variables," and then unclipped a pen from his shirt pocket, commencing to sketch on a napkin, diagramming his objections until Abdul interrupted him.

Broke in gracefully (his mind leaping ahead, having already sorted and stacked both pro and con: each probability weighed, balanced, sacked away like fruit; the facts alone rowing up as in a long equation), taking the engineer's hands (his grip friendly but custodial, just the right pressure, careful as a retriever holding prey in its teeth) to explain exactly how it could be done; the solution (by now filed neatly as a deck of binary cards), one so fantastic yet so simple that he laughed as he began to speak, talking for more than an hour while they fired questions at him (*good* questions, too; so he knew why he'd been called over in the first place: they'd agreed on the tunnel in advance; what they wanted from him was the layout, the works, the pieces assembled as before at the Munich Olympics), ending finally with deference to the engineer. "Would you agree in this way we eliminate your variables?"

By way of congratulations, the engineer had managed a sullen nod.

But afterwards had come the bombing at Machiavelli's and he'd disregarded the tunnel, tucked it away in his memory (who forgot nothing; the plan stored in the vault in sequence like serialed bills, dry and crisp to the last detail) until that evening in the Algonquin when George mentioned the Committee's directive.


"What sort of boat?"

"That's your department." George scooped peanuts from a bowl, shook them in his fist like dice. The owner of a rug-importing firm in Paris, he was one of those small wiry men with Yemeni blood and a nervous appetite. "Whatever you need to do the job."

"This is going to be expensive."

George replied between munches in a peanut-thick voice. "Of course . . . That was understood . . . in your case." Thickswallowing, his Adam's apple bobbed like a cork. "Don't worry about funds; as usual, you have carte blanche."

"A full coffer. How delightful. Courtesy, I take it, of Lufthansa Airlines?" (His lone skyjacking venture—conceived while stroking the cello—which had paid off handsomely to the tune of five million dollars without a shot fired—*as* he'd predicted, who in Berlin as visiting lecturer for one quarter had watched the whole affair unfold on German television, experiencing an *in absentia* participatory thrill not unlike, he fancied, an author seeing his play performed.)

"One thing. They've altered the operation slightly."

"Oh? In what way?"

George toyed with one of the rings on his right hand. "They've selected the Lincoln Tunnel. And it has to be done at a certain time. They want to kill someone in particular inside."

Abdul was amused. "*Slightly*? Thank goodness you're not my tailor, George."

Sober as a Mullah, George leaned forward on his elbows. "Naturally, they wish to know your sentiments."

"That depends. How much advance notice will I have?"

"I'll telephone you as soon as his plane leaves Paris."

"Six . . . *hours*." Abdul said pleasantly. "I volunteered to destroy a tunnel, not walk on water."

George shrugged neutrally. "I just carry messages, Abdul."

"Then take a memo: the Lincoln is a most unfortunate choice. Emphasize unfortunate."

George frowned. "I don't understand. It's a tunnel."

"A tunnel *system*, George."

"All right, dammit, a system. What are you driving at?"

"The Lincoln Tunnel operates *three* tubes instead of two. It is in this respect unique."

"So?"

Abdul smiled patiently. He placed three left-hand fingers palm-down on the table. "Three tubes. Imagine you are looking at them from the New Jersey side. The north tube"—he pointed to the finger on his right—"handles only west-bound traffic leaving New York. The South accommodates those foolish enough or forced by necessity to enter Manhattan in a car. The center tube, however, has several functions. Normally, it relays both east-and-west-bound vehicles, one lane in each direction. In addition, when either of the outer tubes is closed for maintenance, the center tube replaces it. To complicate matters, it serves as a dual auxiliary during rush hours: both lanes open to New York-bound commuters in the early morning, switching over by late afternoon to expedite the four o'clock mass evacuation.'' He paused, but George was still confused, still staring at him with puzzled beady Yemeni eyes. *"So*, in order to trap a specific person driving into New York, we'd have to mine the south *and* center tubes, because there is almost no way, certainly not on six hours' notice, to guarantee which one he would take. Now, the outer tubes present no critical problems as far as demolition is concerned. But due to the proximity of the three roadways, it would be next to impossible to single out the center tube with any degree of accuracy. In fact, we'd stand a good chance of missing it entirely. Do you follow me?''

"Balls," George said gloomily.

"Good. Now cheer up; I said it was unfortunate, not hopeless. Tell me—who is this mysterious *arrivée?*"

George's cupped hand snaked bowlward. "The one-eyed man."

Folding his arms, Abdul leaned back and looked across the room for a moment before he said, "I thought he was off in the Gaza looting Canaanite tombs under the guise of Archeology."

"No. He's in Tel Aviv writing his memoirs."

"Since when do VIPs deplane at Newark International instead of Kennedy?"

"He doesn't know about Newark. The pilot will inform him of the flight-plan change after they pass Halifax."

"Nova Scotia?" Abdul sat up and lit a cigarette. "Perhaps you'd better tell me everything."

George told it quickly.

On October 15th, the conspicuously maimed General was traveling to Paris to receive an award from French Zionists. Initially, there had been some discussion about killing him by mounting a suicide raid on Baron Rothschild's estate, where as usual the recipient would be a guest until his departure. This idea had been abandoned a month ago, however, when, through sources in Tel Aviv (specifically, the microfilm of a letter sent diplomatic pouch from Rothschild to the General) and Washington (in this case, a Pentagon Staff Colonel who had become a compulsive gambler and, after heavy losses, a seller of information), the Organization had uncovered the following facts:

One: the General was flying from Paris to New York under absolute secrecy on October 18th in Rothschild's private jet.

Two: he would be driven from New York to the home of Israel's Ambassador to the UN, where he would confer with top officials from the Departments of Defense and State for the purpose of negotiating a highly classified codicil to the newest U.S.-Israeli pact.

Three: because in return for signing the upcoming peace accord with Egypt, as a price for her painful territorial concessions (the Sinai mountain passes which did not belong to her, the oil fields she had stolen, etc.), Israel had demanded (and would receive, according to the Colonel; the issue being not whether but when) a supply of fissionable plutonium sufficient to enable her to develop full nuclear capability in her research center at Dimona in the Negev Desert.

In short, the Rubicon.

Therefore, ten days ago Rothschild's pilot (an incurably loyal employee named Rene Boule) had been removed in a manner designed to avoid untoward suspicion. As anticipated, Rothschild had replaced Boule with his regular copilot, a man named Straus—an ambitious fellow who, on those occasions when his employer enjoyed immunity from customs, augmented his income by serving as bagman for a Lebanese opium dealer who had ties with The Committee. Threatened with exposure and imprisonment, Straus had agreed to invent a plausible excuse for landing at Newark in exchange for one hundred thousand dollars and sanctuary in Damascus.

Thus the tunnel. Hence Abdul.

"Now," George concluded, "what will you need?"

"Men. *Trained* men. Don't send me amateur fanatics like those idiots who ruined everything at Munich. The qualifications for this job are technical. Five experienced scuba divers, all with proven demolition ability, one of whom speaks English fluently. I'll furnish their equipment here. Once you've selected them, I want their measurements. Get a good tailor to do this. The men themselves have to be in New York no later than the middle of September."

"Fine. We'll locate the men. What else?"

"Contact with this Colonel of yours. That can be arranged?"

"Easily. But I warn you, he's a difficult man, subject to periodic bouts of cold feet."

"Let me handle that."

"I'll see him tomorrow, then. You haven't mentioned money yet."

"Half a million dollars."

George pursed his lips. "That's pretty steep . . ."

". . . plus my fee."

"*Fee?*" George smiled unsurely. "You are making jokes again."

"George," Abdul said gently, "when this is over, the entire Israeli secret service will come after me. I'll have to disappear."

"So? Come to Damascus."

"My friend, there are fifty Israeli agents in Damascus, to say nothing of the CIA men hiding in camel pens. Like the unsuspecting Straus, I'd be dead before my bags were unpacked. No. There is only one impregnable refuge: the Soviet Union."

George shook his head. "Impossible. They wouldn't accept you."

"Russia, George. I want the way clear. A visa—signed, sealed and delivered. Also a place to live in Minsk. And one million dollars, three-quarters to be deposited in a numbered Swiss account, the rest in my New York bank. Before I buy so much as a flipper."

George examined his rings unhappily, as if they might have to go at auction in order to raise the cash. "Why Minsk?"

"I have colleagues there. They will provide support should an attempt be made to remove me. And I hate to be idle."

"I'll see if it can be arranged," George told him guardedly.

"Do that, George. Arrange it. Remind them that I am not one of their *fedayeen*. A sympathizer, yes; but don't expect me to lay my head on the block in the name of Allah."

"Not even for Palestine?"

Abdul placed the glass of cognac over his heart, said mock-seriously: "*Dulce et decorum est, pro patria mori.*" He took a sip before continuing. "During the 1948 hostilities, George, when I was fourteen, my father quartered a group of Iraqi irregulars on our farm outside Nazareth. Twenty-odd un-uniformed fanatics drunk on blood and the Koran: come to Palestine to drive the infidels into the sea. Armed with flintlock rifles and rusty sabers and an ignorance of modern warfare that, if converted to lead, would have sunk an aircraft carrier. They scattered like birds in the face of Israeli artillery—took wing and came to roost in our barn. Because my father, who was not a violent man, was more concerned with harvesting our orchards than with fighting Jews, nonetheless believed it was his patriotic duty to shelter them.

"They stayed in hiding three days: lounging on the straw, pining for Iraq and gorging themselves on our oranges. Having traveled so far to wage *jihad*, however, they were not about to be denied a bloodbath. On the second evening, therefore, first girding their loins with hashish, they marched out to seek the enemy. Several hours later they chanced upon an undefended Israeli farm. They butchered the entire family after raping the mother and her eleven-year-old daughter, then burned the place to the ground. Early the following morning, requisitioning three of our goats and a dozen pullets, they cleared out without saying goodbye.

"That same afternoon an Irgun commando unit led by a one-armed Captain descended on our farm with fixed bayonets. An informer—an *Arab* informer, mark you—had led them to our door. My father could have thrown himself at their feet, pleading that he had been forced to collaborate at gunpoint. But, on the contrary, he refused to tell them anything about the Iraqis.

"And so they hung him, in the barn—tossing a rope over the rafters and pulling him up. The Captain, a handsome fellow with a thin mustache, made my mother and me watch it to the end."

"Your father was a brave man," George said politely.

"He was a fool," Abdul replied. "And his death taught me the folly of allegiance to any cause other than myself. So please do not invoke the Fatherland. My relationship with the Committee is of a contractual nature. I need money. Protection. Point out to them that this may be a rather extended period of seclusion. Suppose I were to run out of funds and the Russians put me to pulling beets on one of their collectives. How long do you think I'd last before some Jewish worker cut my throat? Fix it for me, George."

George laughed softly. "I'm trying to picture you pulling beets. All right, I'll fix it. But what about that business with the center tube?"

"I'll create a diversion to block it temporarily, long enough to insure that our man takes the south entrance."

"How are you going to detonate the bomb at the right moment?"

"*Bombs*, George. We want to *seal* the tunnel: prevent our famous commander from working one of his tactical miracles."

"The *fedayeen* . . ."

". . . Forget the *fedayeen*; they'll be dead before he is. I doubt they'll be able to hold the openings for more than thirty minutes. We have to rely on water to do our killing. So two bombs, George."

"Okay—how do you plan to detonate *two* bombs?"

"Ah," Abdul waved a cautionary finger. "One of the first rules a professor learns is never to reveal the answers until his students have completed the test. Get me the visa, a travel permit, and a government-authorized lease. Then deposit the money and mail me the slips. And *then*, George, we'll talk about the tunnel."

"Be reasonable, Abdul. The Committee will want a few concrete details."

Abdul nodded understandingly. "In that case, tell them . . . crab cages and model airplanes are the secret."

"Crab cages?"

"And model airplanes, George. Tell them that."

# Two

~~

"It just wouldn't work, I'm tellin you," Gunny said irritably to the reporter. He held up both hands as though stilling applause. "Look, there's twelve teevee cameras in each tube, fixed up with mirrors to photograph in both directions. And the way they're spaced, you can follow a car from the time it enters till it leaves. Because they got a setup, man, looks like Walter Cronkite's control room in the administration building."

"Which stands south of the toll booths on the Jersey side," Salvador intervened. "Set back from the roadway on a rise. That's where they keep the computers, see. Got 'em in a big soundproof open room, housed inside a long glass booth stretches down one side. Clickin along like clockwork day and night . . . Why glass? Keeps out dust and heat."

"There's somethin like fifty-six oversized split-screen television monitors on the back wall," Gunny said. "You can watch the inside of all three tunnels at the same time, see both approaches, follow the traffic build-up way up to midtown Manhattan and get a view of the harbor to boot—all without leavin your chair."

Flashing the sigh of victory for emphasis, Salvador said: "Because they got two other camera locations, you know: one a

47

~~

revolvin affair on top a building on the New York side; the second
in a glass cabin mounted over the toll booths at the Jersey entrance.
Inside the cabin (which is nicknamed the Dairy Queen) there's
traffic controllers, checkin their monitors, which're fed by that
revolvin camera across the river in New York.''

''You gotta see it when they're buildin up for the shift,'' Gunny
advised the reporter, ''at the height of the rush hour when commuters're pourin off the island, say an early evenin in the fall like
now—when it's beginnin to get dark and them big commuter
busses're shootin out the portals like torpedos out of a tube and a
solid flow of cars're streamin into Jersey with their lights on: red
and yellow beams of light bendin and bouncin and makin wavy
lines that look like laser beams. . .''

''. . . And suddenly,'' Salvador announced, ''one of them
controllers in the Dairy Queen presses a button on his panel—
closin the east-bound lane of the center tube, see. Because over in
New York traffic has slowed to a crawl, backin up into the city
streets, and there's a pile of cars millin like cattle at the mouth of
the tunnel, nose to tail, horns goin full blast . . .''

''. . . So he presses that button,'' Gunny resumed with his eyes
narrowed on Salvador. ''Back in Jersey nothin's changed except
that that one lane is empty. Looks funny: cars flashin in and out on
either side of that dead space. Looks odd, like it'd been abandoned. There's a lull while the toll girls shift booths, and then a cop
moves the barriers outa the way. After a bit a police jeep comes
drivin out with its lights blinkin to signal that the lane is clear. And
in a matter of seconds, so sudden it's like champagne when you
pop the cork, there's another stream of cars flowin into Jersey.''

''In case you're interested,'' Salvador said, ''the picture on
them teevee monitors in the administration building is clear as a
bell. You can pick out make and model; tell if a man or woman is
drivin; count the occupants; read the license plate number . . .''

''. . . You see a car comin head-on, say, on the right-hand part
of the screen,'' Gunny proposed. ''Real small at first, but gettin
closer and closer and bigger all the time until you can make out the

driver plain as hell. Then it disappears for a fraction, but before you can blink there it is on the left-hand side. . .''

''. . . Blip-blip, just like that,'' Salvador added. ''Only now it's goin away from you, gettin smaller and smaller . . .''

''. . . But by then,'' Gunny lunged for the last word, ''you've picked it up comin towards you on another monitor . . .''

''. . . And if you multiply that by fifty-six,'' Salvador went blithely on, ''times twenty-four hours a day, you get some idea what it's like to sit scannin those tunnel monitors. Imagine watchin the same scene in a silent movie, over and over.''

Gunny waved his empty bottle. ''Imagine gettin us a beer, rubbermouth.''

# Three

~~~

    The registered package arrived ten days later. Inside, Abdul found two envelopes, his new passport (stamped with a Russian visa), and a Russian travel permit. One envelope contained a government-approved, paid-up year's lease on (and keys to, taped to the back of a snapshot of) a dreary-looking house on Pavlov Street in Minsk. The other held a sheet of paper listing the appropriate physical dimensions of the *fedayeen*. (Four were big men, six-footers; the fifth—his English-speaker, he assumed—was only five feet, six inches tall and had the waist of a girl.) Clipped to the paper were two deposit slips (each for three-quarters of a million dollars): One pertaining to a numbered account in Geneva, the second in his name at the Chase Manhattan.

    Having already picked it out, he bought the cruiser, paying $307,492.74. The *Vita-Vita* came well equipped, with almost two of everything, it seemed—from radar, sonar, depth and direction finders down to shower-toilets and watermakers—and so the only extra gear he purchased had been a Danforth standard anchor and three hundred feet of heavy chain, plus one unusual item he delivered personally: twenty gallons of yellow paint (ordered from Japan the day after his conversation with George, a new and most remarkable synthetic which, when applied to metal, hardened to a tough phosphorescent surface), asking the yacht broker to have both chain and anchor given three spray coats. The broker, a bald and garrulous man with close-set, commission-glazed eyes, had nodded coolly as though Abdul's request were natural and wise, sure proof of seamanship. (To cronies later he would say: "Ten percent of three-hundred thou'—you know what I'm talking? Yellow paint he wants, it's his. I offer no discouragement. Waves I do not make. I'm talking thirty grand. Listen, he gives the word I carve his initials on every fucking *link*.")

He shopped for diving gear while the *Vita-Vita* was being outfitted. Based on the fact that October water temperature in the Hudson could drop to a numbing 50° Farenheit, making any lengthy underwater work impossible in conventional wet suits, he chose nylon-lined uni-suits (each tailored individually) made of quarter-inch specially-treated neophrene rubber. Designed in Sweden for scuba operations in the Arctic Ocean, the one-piece garment (which left only the hands and a heartshaped hole over the face exposed) encased a diver in a sac of dry air warmed constantly through body heat. For air tanks he decided on twin-83's equipped with Poseidon regulators. He selected a face mask with a built-in demand valve and exhaust port in order to eliminate the strain of a standard mouthpiece. Then came harnesses, underwater lamps, flippers, insulated three-fingered gloves, knives, weight belts, watches, depth gauges, air pressure gauges—the normal paraphernalia, five complete sets. In addition he bought an air compressor; two single tanks (the smaller 50's, for which a machinist had been hired to forge adapters so that flaring nozzles similar to those on fire extinguishers could be attached to them), and five head lamps. All told, his purchases came to just over seven thousand dollars.

On the 24th of August he paid eight thousand dollars for a reconditioned Land Rover, and then drove the vehicle to a shop that specialized in armor plating. (The foreman grunted with surprise as he went over Abdul's written specifications. At one point he whistled softly and looked up: "Jesus Christ, mister—you expectin a *war*?") On the last day of the month he acquired a used but immaculate black Cadillac limousine for twelve thousand dollars. The car was completely bullet-proof, having been the property of Iran's ambassador to the United States. He parked it in his garage next to the Honda 550 motorcycle he had bought brand-new the day before.

Mooring at the 79th Street Marina, he spent the following seven days on the *Vita-Vita,* testing her equipment and getting the feel of her; at the same time studying the Hudson with the aid of tide and current tables together with a chart of the lower channel (photographically enlarged, the tunnel section magnified four times its size) taped to the control panel in front of the helm—his object not to locate the Lincoln (its course defined as sure as sonar by that ventilation tower standing out from the New York shore) but pinpoint its exact position on the Jersey side: taking multiple daylight fixes (using the distant tower for bearing but triangulating on various tall buildings) and then repeating the procedure at night, gradually narrowing it down, refining his calculations until he was confident that, however moonless or fogbound, he could have harpooned the tunnel with the anchor from either bank.

He met the Colonel on the evening of September 9th.

In the Algonquin once more, after yet another dinner; but remaining upstairs this time in a darkened dining room where old white-haired waiters came and went silently on thick-soled shoes, moving in and out of shadows like uniformed attendant ghosts. The Colonel (middle-aged and martial-looking despite the blue business suit, a handsome Georgian if you didn't mind the thin domineering mouth) ordered Jack Daniels instead of cognac, balancing the tumbler in his fingertips as he drawled: "George" (which came out *Jawdge*) "mentioned military equipment. What exactly did you have in mind?"

Abdul surprised him, ambushed the arrogant "at ease, men" air by handing across a pen and pad. "Write this down, Colonel." He waited until the Colonel, smiling like a resigned indulgent parent, took up the pen. "Two U.S. Navy underwater metal detectors—I want their latest portable model . . . also a pair of those battery-powered boring instruments frogmen use in UDT work, the kind with revolving heads . . . four gas masks . . . two cases of hand grenades, ten concussion grenades in each case . . . four M-16 rifles and four thousand rounds of clip-loaded ammunition . . . five underwater hand lamps, ten thousand candle power capacity . . . two tungsten-halogen underwater lamps, 70,000 centerbeam candle power capacity . . . two 60-pound marine shape charges armed with pentalite plastic explosive, each furnished with three-hundred feet of neophrene-insulated detonating wire.'' He sipped his cognac until the Colonel stopped writing. "That's it.''

Looking down at the list, the Colonel said, "My word, y'all must be planning quite a siege.''

"Any questions?''

"*Well*,'' the Colonel said reluctantly, "those tools are fairly easy to ob*tain*, of course. I do have the proper clearances and the necessary authority. But if I may sug*gest*, there are a dozen comparable devices on the commercial market.''

"I didn't ask for your advice,'' Abdul said pointblank. "Save your opinions for the two-dollar window.''

The Colonel forced a tight-lipped smile. "George told me you were a caustic person. He was right.''

Abdul pointed to the pad. "You have a week, no more.''

"And *you*,'' the Colonel said indignantly, "can go piss up a *rope*. I have no intention of risking my neck to filch a few paltry supplies. *Nor* did I come here to be insulted by . . .''

". . . Save your histrionics for the track, Colonel. You're here because a certain bookie has threatened to break your legs unless you come up with the ready by the end of the month. Also because that namesake of yours is waiting for his tuition check down at . . . good ol' VMI, isn't it? I don't suppose he knows that his old man is in hock up to his holster, or that he's dropped enough in the past year to start a stud farm.'' He raised his empty glass and waved it when he caught the waiter's eye. Turning back, he added, "You're here because you sold out and we bought the title. And you don't have an option clause. A week.''

The Colonel looked as though he were going to be ill. He mustered a lame, defeated smile, that of a man watching his horse finish out of the money in the last race on a bad day. ''That's the trouble with you boys—always impatient. Chop chop. I can't pick up hand grenades and M-16's like bread in a *su*permarket. Explosives mean official *chan*nels. *Pa*perwork. Strict accountability, even for a full Colonel. Ord*inar*ily, I'd have to sign my *name* for those charges. Now, I trust you will appreciate my desire to remain a silent *part*ner in this . . . *en*terprise.''

''Never trust a Bedouin, Colonel.''

''*For*tunately, I know a man who can furnish the weaponry. He's highly reliable. American, of course. A Marine supply-sergeant, in fact, with access to all the warehouses . . .''

''. . . Spare me his pedigree. I don't care who you use, so long as you complete that list.''

''*Un*fortunately, he's a very greedy individual.''

''Most traitors are,'' Abdul said lightly. Reaching down, he slid his briefcase over to the Colonel's chair. ''You'll find thirty thousand dollars in there. That should be sufficient to appease even the most avaricious of supply-sergeants. You'll receive a similar sum upon delivery, which will be as follows.'' He took the pen and pad. ''Once you have all the items, rent a station wagon and call me at this number. I'll tell you where to bring them.'' He tore off the sheet and extended it, but instead of letting go once the Colonel's fingers touched it, he held on, adding: ''Listen to me carefully. I do not like you. So don't foul up. No mistakes and no excuses. You screw me and I'll serve you on a platter to the CIA—tapes, photostats of every document we've bought, the whole shebang as they say in Georgia. Is that clear?''

''Perfectly,'' the Colonel said in a choked voice. ''You needn't worry, however; I have my honor to protect.''

Abdul gave him a bored look. ''Your honor is in that briefcase, Colonel.'' He bent to the pad, wrote for several moments, then glanced up impatiently. The Colonel sat stunned. ''I want to be alone now,'' Abdul said, dismissing him.

Afterwards he made a list of essentials for the party he was throwing on the *Vita-Vita* on September 12th.


Because knowing *how* was only half of it.

The immediate tunnel area, that wide imaginary lane stretching from bank to bank, was a restricted zone close in off the shores, precisely where Abdul intended to sink his charges. During the day, any unauthorized vessel that delayed too long or broke down near either site was sure to be spotted from the ventilation tower on the New York side and quickly ousted or taken in tow by one of the seventeen police boats patrolling the harbor. Without some form of official sanction, he would thus be forced to operate entirely at night for the better part of thirty days, gambling that the harbor police or a passing boat would not discover him—the odds against which were akin to the likelihood of Richard Nixon's effigy being added to Mt. Rushmore.

So to do the job properly, he needed access, needed a front.

Needed a caterer, a bartender, and seven cases of liquor as well. Sent out thirty invitations, ostensibly to celebrate his leave of absence for the coming term. Installed a canvas top over the flying bridge; strung lights fore and aft from the antenna (two drooping lines which took the shape of a pagoda roof); set up a portable bar on the bridge to accommodate browsers. For those who wished to dance on the stern, he hooked the tape deck to the *Vita-Vita*'s hailer.

The 12th was Saturday. It came, declined to a cool evening . . .

\*

*(Music: Stan Getz doing a job on a quiet blues, the notes strong and steady, flawless, rippling occasionally like rustled velvet.)*

*The scene opens with a full view of the* Vita-Vita's *salon as seen through the sliding glass door at the stern. It is midnight; only fifteen guests remain—most of them in groups of twos and threes around the cabin, the party having reached that point where people become more or less stationary.*

*(Throughout we hear the constant buzz of speech and random flurries of laughter, sourceless as the sound of wind.)*

*Sweeping in on a slow zig-zag, the camera lights briefly on various groups; always however, we see (from several angles) figures at the bar at the end of the room–fuzzy at first but coming gradually into focus as in succession we observe:*

*1. An imposing, neatly Vandyked gentleman in his forties standing very close to a young blonde-haired woman who is hanging on his words (which are lost to us, fused with the general hubbub). Caressing her arm, stroking it as one might sleek a cat, his manner suggests the casual savoir-faire of an ambassador from some little European republic, and from her sleepy expression and parted lips we gather that whatever treaty he seeks is in the bag.*

*2. A triangle of two women and a small Chinese man whose crew-cut hair is gray at the tips. One of the women, snub-nosed, a nervous smoker, is talking rapidly, tossing her head to emphasize her point and flourishing her cigarette holder as though casting a string of spells. Raising his hand, the Chinese apparently asks a question, whereupon she thrusts her face to within dental proximity of his to explain, jabbing at will with the holder while the alarmed Chinese dodges her dart-like sallies until, without breaking verbal stride, she resumes her monologue. The other woman, olive-skinned and striking, dressed in an elegant strapless black gown, nods without conviction from time to time. Just now, she turns away and reaches across her face to smooth her long black hair, pausing midway momentarily (the gesture is discreet and cultivated) to stifle a yawn.*

*3. Four graduate students, matched pairs, bunched together on the floor before a couch along the starboard wall. A well-known white NFL lineman-turned-sportscaster occupies the couch, leaning forward with his elbows on his knees as if waiting for the snap, holding forth to the students (who, shiny-eyed, serene and silent, are dividing their attention between him and the miniature water pipe being passed from hand to hand) yet keeping a predatory watch on the darkhaired woman in the black gown, at whom just now he is staring as though she were an opposing tackle.*

*Suddenly the camera veers, closing in on the bar, which snaps into focus: at the port end, two well-groomed young men swung round on their stools discussing some earnest matter; down the bar behind the counter, Abdul: tuxedoed, speaking with the bartender, a good-looking husky Negro. Beaming, Abdul hands the man a hundred-dollar bill, then comes out and takes a stool, swiveling to survey the room. Framed over Abdul's shoulder, the bartender removes his short jacket and stuffs it into a leather bag. Slipping on a sport coat, he steps around and says goodnight to Abdul (who dips his head, tendering a perfunctory smile), then starts across the salon.*

*Reversing the opening sequence, the camera trucks back towards the door. As before, there are blurred figures in the distance—standing outside on the stern, close together, rocking.*

*No one takes notice of the bartender except the olive-skinned woman, who stares with undisguised appraisal as he goes by. Still rattling away, her talkative companion is apologizing profusely to the Chinese, who holds a handkerchief to his ear. Neither remarks the dark-haired woman's departure.*

*She reaches the door as the bartender is sliding it shut. Outside, leaning close, she whispers in his ear, takes his arm. (Meanwhile inside the salon a small comedy unfolds: the lineman-turned-sportscaster, in hot pursuit of the dark-haired woman, wearing a look of anticipation, rather like an old pro about to blind-side a quarterback, freezes in his tracks near the door, frowns, recovers quickly and ambles starboard to inspect the tape deck, glancing sideways warily to see if anyone has witnessed his incompleted pass.) The bartender and the woman walk off, leaving us focused on the figures dancing on the aft deck, who gradually materialize:*

*A short bull of a man moving gracelessly, calling to mind a Hereford attempting locomotion on its hind legs. The pretty face wreathed in red hair above his shoulder is young and dreamily contented: widespread eyes; the nose tilted; a full, strong mouth.*

*Glued together, they turn slowly round and round, not dancing so much as revolving like a door. Now we see the man's face: square-jawed and stubborn, the face of a Marine Drill Instructor, perhaps. Eyes closed, mouth slack with lust. From behind, the girl's ripe body is alive inside a backless green gown: cascading shoulder-length red hair swirling above the sensual roll of her firm buttocks.*

(Note: she is called Christine Dorfmann. Twenty-three years old, born in Amsterdam, she speaks halting, heavily accented English. Earlier Abdul had introduced her to arriving guests as the daughter of an old, dear friend and colleague. She was, he explained, returning to Holland on the 16th, having spent the summer traveling the U.S. During her last three days in this country, Abdul, her quasi-godfather, would have the pleasure of showing her New York.

Her partner is Martin Rugg. Forty-one years old, a divorcé, he teaches marine biology at NYU and is the director of that university's pollution experiments under way now for two years on the Hudson River.

After presenting him to Christine, Abdul had taken Rugg aside, saying: "Look, Marty, I'm going to be awfully busy for the next few hours. Do me a favor and look after Christine. Her English isn't the best, and I don't want her to feel like an outsider."

In somewhat of a state of shock at such a windfall, Rugg had solemnly accepted the charge. And oddly enough she had taken to him (who went about his duties shyly, a grave but diligent chaperon, nearly tongue-tied in the presence of her unconfined, wantonly swelling, incredibly buoyant breasts with their tiny nipples striving to burst the fabric), discouraging the advances of a number of men circling like sharks simply by slipping her arm into his, a move which stimulated Rugg to break out his rusty German, making her laugh at his horrendous pronunciation and thereby shattering what little ice remained between them so that, as the evening wore on, the distance separating their faces, measured by a concerned Abdul coming and going on his rounds, had steadily decreased.)

*

*Now they kiss as the music fades out. A new tune (Hampton Hawes discussing moonlight in Vermont) starts up before they part and enter the salon.*

*Christine pats Rugg's cheek and goes off smiling. Nearing Abdul, who still sits at the bar, she waves. He frowns at her interrogatively. Returning the frown, puffing her lips like an angry fish, she disappears down the companionway ladder.*

*From the side we pick up Abdul carrying a drink, making his way across the cabin to Rugg. Their faces offer a study in contrasts: Abdul, smiling warmly, exuding fellowship, stops to chat for an instant with several different guests; standing near the door, Rugg watches his approach with visible apprehension.*

*Abdul (cheerily)*: The ice-man cometh. (*Handing Rugg the glass*) A good host anticipates his guest's every wish. Scotch, right?

*Rugg (smiling uncomfortably)*: Right.

*Abdul*: I've been wanting to speak with you alone all evening.

*Rugg (dreading the worst)*: It's about Christine, I guess.

*Abdul*: No, of course not. Although I must say you two seem to have hit it off rather well.

*Rugg (quickly)*: She's a hell of a fine girl, Abdul.

*Abdul*: Yes, isn't she? I'm very, very fond of her.

*Rugg (carefully)*: I know you are. That's why I feel so damned . . . (*he grimaces*) . . . Look—if I've stepped out of line, just say the word . . .

*Abdul (shaking his head, placing a hand on Rugg's shoulder)*: . . . Rest easy, Marty. Christine has reached the age of consent, and I'm not a bloody nursemaid. I'm her friend. Yours, too. Actually, I have another favor to ask.

*Rugg (relaxing visibly)*: Yeah? Shoot.

*Abdul*: I want to enlist my services, and that of the *Vita-Vita*, in your research experiments on the Hudson.

*Rugg (takes this in, gives Abdul a quizzical look)*: You're shitting me. You want to use *this* baby to collect bacteria samples?

*Abdul*: Not exactly. I have in mind a project related in a peripheral, hopefully significant way to the overall study NYU is making of the river.

*Rugg (at a loss for words)*: You do?

*Abdul*: A . . . special project. I'd like to study the movement of bottom creatures in the lower channel, say at half a dozen spots, the purpose being to learn what effect, if any, contamination has regarding their presence or absence. In other words, I'd like to see if any conclusions can be drawn between the rise and fall in coloform bacteria levels and crustacean migratory patterns. Does that in any way sound . . . practical?

*Rugg (looks down in concentration for a few seconds, stares hard at Abdul, then smiles)*: Hell, yes. We're conducting similar tests right now with shad and sturgeon. We hadn't even considered shellfish. *(Warming to the idea)*: We could pool your data with ours, maybe even establish some valuable correlations. Our lab people could develop a procedure for testing your samples that might give us an idea of breeding habits, population, an index of their distribution . . . by God, Abdul, it's a damn good idea! Where would you place the cages?

*Abdul*: Ideally, in areas where there would be little or no interference from vessels or fishermen. Two perfect spots would be over the Holland and Lincoln Tunnels, inside the buoys. But I'm afraid the Port Authority and the harbor police would never permit that.

*Rugg (confidently)*: Don't sweat the Authority; they've given me a free hand to run my show. As for the police—I'll clear things with them. All you'll have to do is fill out some forms and put up with a boat inspection. I *will* need a full description of the project in writing, and a diagram of the drop points on a chart. *(Pauses as an idea occurs to him)* There's a council meeting next Tuesday. Could you have the proposal ready by then?

*Abdul (emphatically)*: It will be on your desk Monday morning.

*Rugg (impressed)*: You're really enthusiastic about this, aren't you? *(In a changed voice)* What's it all about?

*Abdul (smiles cocks his head slightly)*: I don't think I understand.

*Rugg (conspiratorially)*: Come on, Abdul. I took Christine on deck. What the hell are you doing with an anchor chain that glows in the dark?

*Abdul*: You opened the windlass cover?

*Rugg*: Christine wanted to see how it worked. Out with it, now—what lies behind this sudden outbreak of civic zeal? Some new grant you've wangled out of Washington? Come on, shipmate, we've known each other a long time, right? Confess.

*Abdul (reluctantly)*: I . . . can't tell you everything, of course. The proposal is still sitting in a Senate subcommittee, and they aren't expected to bring it to the floor before next month. This is therefore in the strictest confidence. In sum, I've designed and submitted a plan for measuring penetrating cosmic radiation from a station on the ocean floor. It's something I've been working on for more than ten years. That's really about as far as I can go.

*Rugg (embarrassed, deflated)*: It's far enough. I'm sorry I stuck my big nose in your windlass.

*Abdul*: No harm done. I meant to tell you eventually, as soon as the Senate officially confirmed my grant. And let me be perfectly honest: there are certain procedures, theories perhaps would be a better word, along with a fair amount of special equipment, that I am anxious to test in the Hudson. If that sounds underhanded, I can only give you my word that these tests would in no way interfere with the shellfish project, which would be carried out in a legitimate and professional manner.

*Rugg (signals for Abdul to stop by sealing the rim of his glass with a flat palm)*: Enough said. I'll tell the council that one of the most respected physicists in the world, a former adviser to the Atomic Energy Commission, who's had more National Science Foundation grants than my entire department, who knows the Hudson, is an accomplished boatman, and the best amateur marine biologist I've ever encountered—this fellow wants to conduct a minor but integral study of the river which promises to enrich our sadly deficient ecological understanding of that septic tank, said study to be financed independently by the aforementioned physicist. Once they learn you aren't going to cost them a penny, the council may name a park after you. Therefore (*saluting Abdul with the glass, he sips*) I drink to your success. (*Squinting one eye*) But I'd give a lot to know what that yellow anchor chain is all about.

*Abdul*: I guarantee you'll be one of the first to know, Marty.

*

(*The Modern Jazz Quartet, low and mellow in the background.*)
*Abdul is kneeling, lighting the water pipe for one of the female students. Rising, he looks around the room, frowns. Collecting several glasses, an ash tray, he goes to the bar. Next, trying to appear casual, he descends the companionway ladder.*

*We follow him down the narrow corridor and into the master stateroom: empty, several coats on the bed. The bathroom likewise is empty, but as he straightens a towel a muffled cry from the adjoining room catches his ear.*

(*Suddenly John Coltrane bursts onto the tape, hard and driving.*)
*Abdul comes back into the corridor and listens at the door to the forward berth.*

*Christine's sharp bird-like cries and Rugg's harsh breathing rise above the music. We hear her moan, a low drawn-out plea that shrinks into an excited gasping staccato matching the beat of his urgent pumping, their voices rising and falling like some primitive song composed of unintelligible mmm's and ahhh's and quick painful grunts, a guttural, asthmatic language in tempo with their thrusting, the sound of flesh drumming flesh coming faster and faster as, with Coltrane, they close toward climax.*

*His face clouded, Abdul goes back upstairs. He plants himself at the top, a smiling sentinel.*

(*George Shearing weaves a moody piano for the wee hour of morning.*)

*Abdul stands in the doorway, saying goodbye to the students.
The salon is empty except for Christine and Martin Rugg, who
stand in close conference near the bar. Now they move apart, Rugg
going below while Christine comes over to Abdul.*

*Abdul*: You disappoint me. That business downstairs was not
part of our agreement.

*Christine (offering him a blasé smile)*: The agreement was to
please him, no? I assure you, he was delighted. *(She shrugs to
underscore her next sentence)* He wants to take me to his apartment. I am supposed to be, how you say, paving the road. He is
very worried about your reaction.

*Abdul*: Stay with him. Call me every evening, in his presence,
just as though you were a dutiful godchild. As for the rest, we
discussed what you have to do.

*Christine*: And afterwards?

*Abdul*: I'll come with him to see you off at the airport. Then you
can forget about this episode and return to your regular clients. I'm
told some are quite famous.

*Christine (sneers)*: Germans. They take me to Spain. A
bullfight, a fancy crucifix. Like all men, they are more generous
when they have no pants on. *(She smiles to herself)* This one is a
little *toro* in bed, and on top of that you pay me what it takes six
months to earn. Besides, New York is more exciting than Madrid.

*Abdul (sees Rugg come up the stairs)*: Make sure that you earn
your money. *(Smiling fondly for Rugg's benefit, but in a flat voice)*
New York can be a very dangerous city.

# Four

"It's all a question of vibrations," Salvador declared. "Them computers're connected to sensors they got under the pavement. Eighteen in each tube, one every three hundred feet or so—strung out mainly in the center mile that's under the river. In a manner of speakin, the sensors control everything."

"Specifically, they're photoelectric detectors called induction loops," Gunny said importantly. "Coiled, like bedsprings, under the roadway. Kind've like a nervous system. They transmit impulses—measurin the volume of traffic by registerin vibrations and sendin split-second messages to the computers, which decipher the information and relay it to the ventilation towers while at the same time adjustin the rate of flow by increasin or decreasin the interval between vehicles by means of the traffic lights."

Salvador poured some whiskey into his beer and passed the half-pint to the reporter. "If you're like me and don't know shit from Sylvania about high-powered electronics, it all sounds pretty complicated. But the principles're simple.

"For example, it stands to reason when there's more cars there's more fumes, and so you gotta change the air faster, gotta speed up the fans . . ."

64

". . . Which're gigantic," Gunny said. "Eighty-six in all, big as a boat each one. Half're blowers that force cold air into the tunnel through ducts along the curbing. Then, as the air warms and rises, it gets sucked out the ceilin grates by the other half, which're called exhausters. The fans're so powerful they recycle the air inside each tube every ninety seconds . . . *What?*"

Salvador laughed, sounding like a startled parrot. "Put a bomb in the *air* shaft?"

"No way," Gunny told the reporter. "In the first place, it ain't a shaft. There's two air chambers: one above the roadway, one below, both runnin the length of the tube. Big enough to walk in, too, except it'd be almost impossible to get inside. The cameras, remember? The cops. But even if you *could* manage somehow to get inside, the noise'd drive you deaf and you couldn't stand up with them fans goin full speed. Seventy miles an hour, pal. Like a damn hurricane, and comin from both directions—because they got ventilation towers on both sides of the river . . . Sure, I been inside. Round, lined with metal. Like being inside a giant rifle barrel. Even with the fans turned down low the air screeches like . . . *Trap*doors?"

"No, no trapdoors," Salvador assured the reporter. "There's passageways linkin all three tubes at each end, but the cops guard those entrances. Only authorized workmen're allowed inside the chambers, and a cop always goes along. And if by some miracle you did manage to sneak past the cops, there'd still be the fans. Gunny ain't kiddin; nobody could buck that wind. Bounce you around like a pebble in a riverbed." He deadpanned a wink. "Blow the hair clean off your balls."

Gunny stood, gathering the empty bottles. "So it couldn't be done from the inside. Too much security; too many eyes. Plus it'd take an atom bomb to lift that riverbed outta the way. And I already explained why it'd be next to impossible to do from the outside. The Hudson. Forget how much money it'd take, how much skill, the equipment (and believe me you ain't got any *idea* how much equipment you'd need to find and mine that tunnel), the harbor patrol, them Port Authority cameras—for*get* all that; just consider the river. You can chart the currents, their set and speed, predict the tides, sure; but we're talkin about the *bottom*, not the top. And down there, where there's swirls and eddies whippin around like a roller coaster between them two main currents; down deep where they all collide and the aftershock can generate a whirl that rolls from bank to bank like storm winds bouncin back and forth in a mountain valley; on the bottom, man, ain't *no*body can predict how the river'll act, which raises the odds against an outside job so high you'd have to hire Jacques Cousteau just to have a *chance*. So once and for all, let's knock off this nonsense about blowin up the tunnel, okay?''

Laying the matter hopefully to rest, Salvador proposed a toast: "I'll drink to *that*.''

# Five

~

*Symptomatic of 28 days, this montage:*

*September 15th*
Dusk. The Colonel drives north along the Hudson Parkway in a blue Volvo station wagon, glancing occasionally at the river: gray now in the dying light, its broad back ruffled with whitecaps licked up by a steady northern breeze.

At the marina parking lot, Abdul directs the Colonel into a slot near the *Vita-Vita* and then ushers him on board across a short gangplank. They go past two husky, hard-looking men (dressed like morose identical twins in brand-new blue jeans, sneakers, and black turtleneck sweaters) who exchange looks with Abdul while the Colonel takes in the cramped aft deck: six large metal cages stacked three-on-three along the port rail; a half-full water barrel at the base of which lie a set of air tanks and a portable air compressor.

Inside at the bar, Abdul and the Colonel chat over coffee as a young man rises behind the counter holding a bottle of *Carlos V* brandy. Slender and pretty as a girl, with long black hair and a delicate face dominated by huge, long-lashed brown eyes, he looks barely eighteen. After pouring the brandy, he goes below. The two

~

twins enter the salon (untidy, scuba gear cluttering the port side), each carrying a shape charge by its leather strap.

Later, one of the twins struggles into the salon with a case of hand grenades balanced on a hand dolly. The Colonel, still sitting at the bar, checks his wristwatch impatiently. Abdul drops a thick envelope on the counter. Without opening it, the Colonel stuffs it into his coat pocket. Abdul goes behind the counter to pour them each another cup of coffee. As he is filling the Colonel's cup, the same twin as before enters with the canvas-bound rifles.

Outside, the other twin is replacing the Volvo's right front hubcap. Several wrenches and a plastic tube lie on the pavement beside him.

Later, both *fedayeen* enter carrying ammunition boxes. The one who has been absent nods to Abdul.

Afterwards on the Hudson Parkway, the Colonel drives south in heavy traffic, listening to the following conversation in his mind:

"You have charming companions, I must say."

"They are what you'd call the 'muscle.' "

"Killers, you mean."

"If you prefer. But highly specialized, as assassins go."

"I'm sure. Tell me, just what are you and your specialists planning to *do* with all this hardware?"

"More coffee?"

"Very well, I'll withdraw the questions." (*After a bit.*) "It's taking your boys an inordinate time, I declare."

"They won't be much longer." (*There is the sound of the envelope falling on the counter.*) "Why don't you count it while we wait?"

"That won't be necessary. I trust you."

"As I said before, Colonel, never trust a Bedouin."

There is a sharp report, as of a tire blowout, and the Volvo swerves violently to the right. In the few seconds remaining to him, the Colonel hears Abdul's echoing voice:

". . . never trust a Bedouin . . ."

Careening out of control, the Volvo explodes. Flames envelope the cab.

\*

### September 16th

Early that afternoon Abdul and Martin Rugg stand with Christine in a waiting room at Kennedy Airport. Long faces on the lovers. The other passengers begin filing out. Abdul kisses Christine on both cheeks, gives her a bear hug, and moves off conscientiously. A tearful Christine embraces Rugg. One last wild kiss, then she flees past a sympathetic stewardess.

Later in the taxi Rugg hands Abdul a thin sheaf of official-looking papers. Abdul reads; looks up suddenly with a big smile on his face; thanks Rugg exuberantly. Clearly enjoying it, Rugg objects.

\*

### September 18th

Morning in the *Vita-Vita* salon. Diving equipment scattered like debris along the starboard walls; food-spattered paper plates on the floor in front of a small projection screen hanging on the port wall. Both galley sinks piled with dishes; dirty glasses dotting the bar; a pot on the stove containing the unwholesome-looking remains of what appears to be chowder.

A telephone rings:

"Hello, George. How gauche of you to call collect."

"Our friends are most upset about the Colonel's unfortunate demise, Abdul."

"It was unavoidable, George. Ask any actuary: indecisiveness and a tendency to gamble recklessly make for a poor driving risk. Quite frankly, I no longer trusted him behind the wheel."

"They wish you had informed them of his condition beforehand. They feel the accident might have been averted had you followed customary procedure."

"There wasn't time, George. The man was dangerous."

"Granted. But also nearly impossible to replace."

"Omelets and broken eggs, George. You can't have one without the other."

"Our friends strongly recommend that in the future you consult with them before making such irrevocable decisions."

"I understand. *C'est tout?*"

"Not quite. They wanted to know if you had paid that final installment to the Colonel."

"Of course."

"In cash?"

"Naturally."

"The idea of counterfeit bills never crossed your mind?"

"That isn't my style, George."

"It wasn't your money, either."

"Carte blanche, you said—remember?"

*

*September 21st*

Morning at the marina. A policeman wearing his regulation face boards the *Vita-Vita*. He walks with Abdul across the salon (once more neat, tastefully arranged), inspects the galley appliances, then goes below, pausing near the bottom of the ladder to check the built-in washer and dryer. He opens lockers in the corridor, revealing sundry gear. Both the master stateroom and the forward berth are orderly and empty. Returning upstairs, he lifts the hatch concealed in the salon carpet and climbs down to inspect the engine room: crammed with gleaming machinery. Next he mounts to the bridge where he discusses navigational equipment with Abdul. Suddenly he smiles and flips his notebook shut.

Later at the bar the policeman sits on a stool beside Abdul. Behind the counter, the attractive young man is pouring coffee into their cups. The officer removes his hat. The young man leans down and slides back the door, exposing several rifles, the case of hand grenades, one of the shape charges, and the bottle of *Carlos V* brandy. He reaches for the brandy.

*

### September 22nd

Night. Slits of light shine through the curtains in the *Vita-Vita*'s cabin. Inside, Abdul stands beside the projection screen on which slides appear each time he presses the remote control device in his hand. He is lecturing to the assembled *fedayeen*, who sit starboard on the floor. A succession of images appear: an exterior shot of Newark Airport; various pictures of the route from there to the turnpike and from thence to Interstate 495. We see the marshes, roadsigns, then the tunnel entrance. Then several interior shots of the first hundred yards, including the spot where the lane bends, to which Abdul points. Holding an imaginary steering wheel, he wrenches it a half-turn. The scarred man interrupts to ask a question. Nodding, Adbul thumbs the slide-change, backing the pictures up until the New Jersey entrance appears.

*

### September 23rd

Morning at the New Jersey entrance to the Lincoln Tunnel. An attractive Puerto Rican girl is watching the Cadillac limousine pull away from her toll booth. Once into the tunnel, the four *fedayeen* appear as silhouettes inside the car. Up ahead the wall begins to curve. As the limousine goes into the bend, the scarred man turns to those in the back, rising in his seat to imitate jerking the steering wheel. The trip through the tunnel is fast and eerie, a blur of lights and unclear images. Hitting the incline, the Cadillac seems to leap toward the curving exit. Just then, however, the driver takes his right arm from the wheel and gives a tug as though he were ringing a bell. Exiting, one of the men in back stares at his diving watch, noting the elapsed time on a pad.

*

*September 25th*

Dawn at the marina. Soft blue light filters through the *Vita-Vita*'s sliding glass door. Facing aft inside the dim salon, arranged in two ranks, the *fedayeen* are praying: their faint invocations, spoken in unison, seem one low murmuring voice. Front to back, the twins and the bearded man; behind them the boy and the one with the mutilated face. (The twins do not resemble one another except in stature. The one on the left with the massive head and broken nose is Moussa. Behind him, lantern-jawed and angular, his head shaved to the skull, stands Mohammed. The bearded man is named Ahmed; the boy, Ali. The scarred man has no name.) They stand with their elbows out, thumbs hooked behind their ears, fingers splayed and trembling. Running their hands slowly down the front of their bodies, they fall on their knees, still reciting, and place their foreheads to shawls spread on the carpet.

*

*September 28th*

Morning. The *Vita-Vita* floats near a tall harbor buoy on the New Jersey side. In the background, looming large, stands the ventilation tower. Abdul is at the stern watching Ali operate a small davit hoist. In the water beside the cruiser a yellow-painted cage disappears, falling through murky blackness. Hitting bottom it sends up a cloud of silt.

Fifteen feet away a large underwater lamp is clamped to the ring of the huge sinker block anchoring the channel buoy. Wavy light outlines a slimy bottom, undulating tentacles of seaweed. In the distance, four divers swim into view; working against the current, propelling themselves with their flippers. They move in pairs, skimming the vegetation. One man on each team holds an underwater lamp and what appears to be a long, phosphorescent spear.

Wearing head lamps, their partners push yellow-glowing metal detectors resembling tremendous lollipops.

Suddenly a diver drops to his feet, the metal detector he holds emitting a shrill sound. He raises his hand, stabs a finger downward, and takes the underwater lamp from his partner, who lifts the spear (a yellow bar some nine feet long, fitted with grapnel-like hooks at one end) and drives it into the mud. Removing a large mallet from his belt, he begins hammering the bar deep. Behind them an irregularly spaced row of similar stakes stretches for some thirty feet like a chest-high, crooked, freshly painted picket fence.

Meanwhile, on the surface, Abdul and Ali at the stern wave to a police boat churning past. The officer on the bridge returns their greeting. He grins as Abdul holds up a large lobster, its claws twisting sluggishly.

*

*October 1st*

Abdul and Ali, both in black tie, sit at a table in Abdul's club on East 67th Street. Lifting his wine glass, Abdul offers a toast, staring across with a direct, speculative smile. Ali meets his eyes, then looks down, and begins sawing at his steak.

At the same time, on the *Vita-Vita*, a disgusted Ahmed spits a mouthful of French fries back into the McDonald's bag and hurls it at the sink. Opening a Big Mac carton, he sniffs, lips curling with contempt, and draws back to send it after the French fries, but Mohammed (coming up from behind to execute a deft "Statue of Liberty") snatches the container from his hand and rejoins the other *fedayeen* on the salon floor in front of the projection screen.

Later, Ahmed operates the slide-changer while the others finish their meal. At the moment they are watching shots of the route to be followed from Interstate 495 to the tunnel. The scarred man is doing most of the talking. He points to a billboard advertising Kent cigarettes which stands near the ramp leading down to the tunnel entrance. There is some discussion, after which he motions to Ahmed for the next slide. Looking bored, Ahmed presses the button, but to his dismay a series of scenes begin snapping by in rapid succession. He punches another button, managing only to shift the stampede in reverse. By now the others are howling. Mohammed tosses a cushion, striking Ahmed aside the head. Ahmed rises, dropping the slide-changer as if washing his hands of its treachery: immediately the pictures begin reeling out in the opposite direction. Enraged, Ahmed kicks the device, whereupon the motion ceases, leaving all of them staring at a long shot of the ventilation tower on the New York side.

*

*October 4th*

A white policeman, lunch pail in hand, wearing the Port Authority uniform, approaches the entrance to the ventilation tower on the New York side. Inside, a Negro policeman watches the officer's approach on closed-circuit television. The white policeman takes the elevator to the top of the tower and enters his office: vending machines to the left of the entrance; computers running the length of the right side; two desks in the far left corner; one large window taking up most of the back wall. Setting his lunch pail on a desk, the policeman goes to the window, through which can be seen the nearby shape of the *Vita-Vita* riding at anchor near the Manhattan shore. He glances casually at the boat, then walks to his desk.

*

*October 7th*

The Cadillac limousine sits in front of the main lobby at Newark Airport. Moussa comes walking out, carrying a briefcase and dressed in a gray suit. Ahmed, wearing a robin's-egg-blue chauffeur's uniform, gets out of the driver's seat and comes around to open the front door. Moussa makes a sarcastic face, pointing to the back door. Furious, Ahmed slams the front door, jerks open the back. Patting him on the cheek, Moussa climbs in.

A few minutes later the limousine speeds down Interstate 495 across from the marshes, following Mohammed in a rented car. The Land Cruiser waits on the shoulder below a large billboard on the right advertising Canadian Club whiskey. As Mohammed and the limousine go past, the scarred man guns the Land Cruiser onto the highway. Following Abdul's plan, the Land Cruiser passes the limousine and pulls in ahead of the rented car. Maintaining their tandem formation, the vehicles proceed to the toll gates, where, one-by-one (the Land Cruiser first, then Mohammed in the target car, and finally the Cadillac limousine) they disappear into the Lincoln Tunnel.

*

*October 9th*

Ahmed sits with a towel around his shoulders staring at Ali, who is trimming his beard. Taking up a razor, Ali beings dry-shaving the thick bristles while Ahmed grimaces. After a bit Ali pauses to strop the razor. Smiling, Ahmed reaches out slyly to stroke the boy's genitals. Ali glances at the hand, then clips it with the razor, drawing blood. As Ahmed starts to rise in anger, Ali places the blade against his throat. Wide-eyed, attempting to see over his chin, Ahmed sinks back in the chair. Ali regards him with a calm expression. In a few moments he resumes shaving under Ahmed's watchful, smoldering eyes.

*

*October 10th*

Ali stands on the roadway above the New Jersey portals, looking down at the line of cars coming and going. The Honda rests nearby on its kickstand. He opens his brown leather jacket to speak into a walkie-talkie hanging in a pouch, then switches to receive and bends his head to listen.

Abdul stands on the uncovered bridge of the *Vita-Vita*, wearing a thin wire-frame headset with a button speaker on the end of a crescent-shaped stem that curves around his cheek. Looking at his watch, he frowns and says something angrily.

*

*October 12th*

Morning on the *Vita-Vita*. The *Times* folded before him on the table, a drowsy Abdul sips coffee on the covered bridge. At the rear of the bridge Ali is lying naked on his stomach on the cot. Spreading the paper, Abdul rubs his eyes. Suddenly he pauses, noticing a headline. Leaning forward, he reads, a smile growing across his face. Rising quickly, he goes below and picks up the telephone.

"George? *Bonjour, mon ami.*"

"Abdul, do you know what time it is in Paris?"

"I bear tidings of great joy, George."

"Two o'clock in the morning."

"*Un pue de chose*, George. Perk up—I'm going to read you an announcement appearing in today's *New York Times*. I quote from the headline: 'Port Authority to close Lincoln center tube for repairs.' "

"Abdul, if this is a joke . . ."

"I continue: 'The director of the Port Authority of New York and New Jersey disclosed last night that the Lincoln Tunnel's center tube would be closed for emergency repairs for seven days beginning October 15. According to director Alexander Bly, the center tube, oldest of the three roadways, has been the source of constant motorist complaint for the past several months because of water seepage and numerous chuckholes . . . Are you listening, George?"

"Yes, yes. Please go on."

"Let's see . . . Bly attributed the vibration damage and concrete deterioration to outmoded construction methods of the 1930s . . .

blah-blah-blah . . . citing history of shutdowns for costly night repairs . . . blah-blah-blah . . . an entire resurfacing necessary if roadway is to be maintained safe for vehicles . . . unpopular decision, but inevitable considering circumstances . . . employing new method recently tested successfully on tunnel under Thames . . . strain on city's commuter population regrettable but unavoidable and, on the bright side, only temporary . . . an inconvenience New Yorkers will without question weather as so often other storms in the past . . . time will prove it was right choice in long run . . . see page three for maps outlining suggested alternate routes for commuters . . ."

"We're in the clear, then?"

"Home free, George. Thanks to the city of New York."

# Six

~

The Interrogator (this in London on the morning of October 26th after it was all over), a scholarly-looking Israeli bent over a loose-leaf notebook (receding hair, horn-rim glasses, sallow skin), did not look up as George was led into the room.

Nor when George sat down in front of his (the Interrogator's) desk in a high-backed wooden chair of most unusual construction (the center of the seat felt like metal; there were three square metal plates bolted flush at intervals along the top of each arm rest, a like number checkering the forepart of the front legs; and two oversized metal footrests resembling treadles on old-fashioned sewing machines).

Nor while the guards strapped George's arms and legs and feet down tight.

Nor after one of them drew a damp line across his forehead with a cotton applicator (the liquid was acidic, its pungent odor strongly present for a second and then gone), leaving George mystified but otherwise unharmed.

Did not look up, but rather turned a page and motioned for the guards to leave.

Read on without reacting when George, whose head (swathed in a grimy, blood-stained bandage) was splitting, said in a parched voice, "I'm hungry."

~

Turned another page.

"*Hey.*" (This stab at indignation set off spots before his eyes.) "I haven't had anything to eat since your men kidnapped me." His eyes traveled the room. "Where in the hell *am* I, anyway?"

Even then did not look up. But spoke (in a smooth, persuasive, low-keyed voice): "Appre*hen*ded. One kidnaps an innocent person. You are a criminal, a fugitive from justice—wanted in the United States for mass murder, also by the French in connection with the slaying of Rene Boule. We simply took you into protective custody."

George made a stab at contempt (managing a mirthless croak that sent pain slashing through his head)—"Protective, my ass. Your boys break into my room in Lisbon, knock me on the head, drug me, fly me God knows where . . . I spent the last three nights tied to a bed (no blanket, not even a pillow, nothing but a pot to piss in), answering questions during the day, fourteen hours at a clip without a break (*they* took the breaks: whenever one got tired another took his place; me, I just sat there bleeding), no nourishment, only that miserable paint remover someone fortified with coffee . . . so we both know why I'm fastened to this barber's chair; don't disguise it as legality." He glanced down at his fetters, made a wry face. "What do you do with the *healthy* prisoners—bind them in chains?" He shifted in his seat, regretting it straightway as the dizziness engulfed him. Closing his eyes he said weakly, "I need a doctor. Aside from starving me to death, I think you bastards fractured my skull."

Looked up at last: removed his glasses to wipe the lenses with a handkerchief. Said cordially, "A minor concussion, nothing more. You were treated by a doctor on the flight from Lisbon. He administered the drugs and prescribed a liquid diet. The coffee tastes odd because it contains medicine. You should be well enough to eat some solid food before the day is out. In the meantime, I have a few additional questions to ask. Once you have answered them your troubles will be over."

George groaned (one part pain, the other pure exasperation)—

"Look, I've talked so much the last two days, my *gums* are swollen."

Replaced his glasses (worn low on a long nose) and smiled over the rims like a benevolent schoolmaster. "It may interest you to know that we contacted the authorities in Paris and the U.S. in an effort to confirm your deposition. To put it mildly, the results have been extraordinary. The French police, under the command of a detective named Rousseau, were fortunate enough to locate and capture two of the killers you hired to do away with Boule. The third, the ringleader, it seems, was murdered two months ago in a gangland vendetta. Detective Rousseau, quite naturally, expressed his eagerness to meet you and the girl. Especially the girl. For some mysterious reason, he was overjoyed to learn of her existence."

"Why not? After all, being Palestinian, she qualifies as an endangered species."

"Also half-French, I believe you said." Leafed through the notebook, found the place, continued: "Yes . . . and teaching in an elementary school in Cairo." Peeked over the rims to add: "An unusual occupation for a murderess."

"Really?" George said through his teeth. "What was *your* occupation before you joined Mossad?"

Dipped his head in tribute—"*Touché.*"

"Tell Rousseau to forget the girl. I offer you the same advice. Egypt will never extradite her to France. And Cairo isn't Lisbon. In order to take *her* into protective custody, you'll have to start another war."

The Interrogator's smile had frost on it. "Frankly, Boule's death is of only marginal interest to us. The bombing in New York, of course, is primarily an American problem, one they were almost at a loss to unravel, I might add, until we passed a copy of your testimony detailing Nosser's remarkable plan to the CIA—who promptly leaked it to the *New York Times*, which produced a scandal of Watergate proportions overnight. Reporters overwhelmed the Pentagon. They dug up the corpse of that colonel along with a live sergeant who sold weapons to the underworld, and then dove headfirst into the hole after more treasure. So far, they have unearthed a homosexual ring and a brigadier general whose townhouse was paid for by the South Korean government. The disclosures in New York were no less sensational. As a result, Congress convened at midnight, ordering an immediate investigation of the Pentagon, the Port Authority, and New York University. Your Mr. Rugg, by the way, committed suicide in his cell yesterday.''

"Too bad," George said indifferently.

Chuckled once, deep in his throat, without altering that wintry smile. ''To come to the point, our main objective is to identify your other associates on the Committee. Imagine my dismay, then, to learn that you cannot recall who they are.''

"My memory must have been impaired by the concussion," George submitted.

Leaned forward on his elbows; formed an umbrella with his fingertips. "Perhaps. Nevertheless, you are the only person alive who can tell us their names and whereabouts. I suggest you concentrate. Now.''

"No dice," George balked. "I'm not talking until I've had something to eat.''

Picked up with his right hand what George took to be a hand calculator, saying: "I urge you to reconsider that decision.''

"Up yours.''

Dipped his head once more and replied, "As you wish.''

And without further ado thumbed the voltage regulator (watching without interest as George lunged against the straps with a strangled gasp expelled like steam between teeth clamped tight by the current that bent his body like a bow and held it taut while his eyes bulged and mucus boiled from his nose), releasing it eight seconds later to light a cigarette (while George crumpled over, head lolling to one side, choking on the ropy mucus and urinating in his trousers, his glazed eyes fluttering) which he smoked in silence for half a minute (marking time while George's twitching subsided) before he went on (his voice scarcely audible at first to George, who came alive in agony as the shock wore off, wanting to scream but finding his tongue heavy as lead): "Do not try to move or speak just yet. The motor reflexes usually take longest to come round. Your vision will return to normal shortly. . . . And now let me put you in the picture. The Americans, who want you desperately, have exerted considerable pressure on my government, which has instructed me to turn you over to their representatives this afternoon. If you cooperate, I shall honor those instructions and you will be taken to New York, where expert medical care, good food, and comfortable accommodations abound. All I ask in return are a few names and addresses. But please, do not try my patience any further. We are pressed for time; should you therefore elect to remain obstinate, I shall gladly fry you to a cinder."

George opened his mouth several times. In the end he capitulated with a nod.


"Splendid," the Interrogator said later. "Now—I want to know how they planted the bombs."

"I thought you said we'd be finished once I gave you the names and addresses."

The Interrogator shrugged. "I lied."

"Can I have another cup of coffee?" George ventured.

"Afterwards."

"Dry trousers?"

"Don't impose on my good nature."

George sighed wearily. "All right. Where do you want me to start?"

"Somehow the beginning leaps to mind."

George cleared his throat slowly. "They set the first charge," he said at last, "on the New Jersey side on October sixteenth. By chance, the weather came to their assistance. Late that afternoon a freak Canadian cold front blew into Manhattan. The temperature in Times Square had dropped to thirty-six degrees by ten-thirty . . ."

". . . I am interested in details, not the meteorology report."

". . . It was of course much colder on the Hudson," George added lamely.

*

. . . A northwesterly stirred the surface into scaly ripples. Low fog hanging in the air like a spell. From mid-river came the prolonged and flatulent hornblast of a tug towing a barge upstream with the current: two dim wallowing ghosts barely defined in the flickering glow of the topmost bow-and-stern lights. Some three hundred yards west of the tug the *Vita-Vita* motored downstream along the Jersey shore: her white hull merging with the vapor seeping over her decks, running lights extinguished, the bridge dark except for stray moonbeams and the greenish-blue glare from the radar screen, its periodic bleep punctuating the soft telegraphic clicking of her instruments—both sounds muted by the steady drone of the engines and the river's smooth hiss as it furrowed beneath the keel. Pier lights loomed to starboard like distant smoky nebulae. The multi-colored skyline at the tip of Manhattan was approaching inch by inch off the port bow. . . .

*

"Granted that the fog was a blessing," said the Interrogator, "still it must have presented a substantial problem, even with instrumentation."

George shook his head (which to his astonishment no longer ached)—"Abdul had made allowances for fog by programming a preset course into the computerized direction finder. Any deviation was corrected instantly by the hunting apparatus built into the automatic pilot. In this way he eliminated the necessity of relying on the ventilation tower for alignment. Although the tower was probably visible, sticking out of the fog like a lighthouse. It *was* his lighthouse, so to speak. Once past it, he shifted to manual control."

*

. . . Punching the button to release the automatic pilot, he gunned the engines, swinging the cruiser hard about to port, her bow lifting in a rush as she came churning around and then lowering suddenly as he reduced speed, causing her to pitch slightly as he headed back upriver toward the tunnel . . .

\*

"He made the turn," George said, "at approximately eleven o'clock. The divers were already dressed and sweating inside their rubber suits. They worked in pairs in the salon . . ."

". . . In the dark?"

"No—all the lights were on. The windows and doors had been painted black and covered with tarpaulin. (They *could* have done it in the dark, you know; by then it had become a kind of tandem drill, a mechanical operation: going over each other's clamps and hoses and fittings and straps, while Ali made a last-minute inspection of the special equipment.) Abdul called down over the ship's intercom for a final time check less than a minute after he came out of the turn. According to plan, Ali then left the cabin and went forward to the windlass—no mean feat in all that fog. After that, it was a matter of waiting."

"For Abdul to maneuver into position."

"No—he was already in position. They had to wait three minutes for the river."

"The river?"

George displayed a knowing smile. "They haven't figured that one out in New York, have they?"

\*

. . . Three minutes.

Because at precisely 11:05 P.M. (based on forty days of systematic measure of the currents in the tunnel area) he had calculated that slack water would commence.

Because tidal rivers change direction as a rule four times a day, slack water being the interim between these alternating currents—the time it takes for each new opposing flow to gain maximum speed, which can vary from a few minutes to several hours.

Because despite New York City's cooperation, his plan would not have worked had it not been for this lull—the divers could not have swum (much less have spent thirty days staking out the targets) against an average current speed well above two knots.

And because this night from the onset of slack water, the ebbing Hudson would not exceed 0.4 knots in the vicinity of Thirty-eighth Street until 11:51 P.M.—which gave the *fedayeen* roughly forty-six minutes of relatively calm water in which to plant the charge . . .

\*

"Tell me about this special equipment."

George made a stab at discouragement. "I never really saw the items. Abdul described them to me during one of his reports, that's all."

"Nonetheless."

"They were taking along a boring tool," George said irritably, "—a battery-powered, T-shaped affair something like a jack-hammer with four curved blades radiating like spokes from the end of the shaft. And one of the extra air tanks, modified so that it could be used for excavation."

"In what way modified?"

"All I know for certain is that there was a nozzle, similar to those plastic funnels on fire extinguishers, attached to the nose. Mohammed carried the thing on top of his regular harness, which had also been modified: fitted with two steel hoops that must have been adjustable because I believe they slid the tank through the hoops and then snaplocked them in place into grooves notched in the canister shell."

"Nothing else?"

"A few small tools, all very ordinary."

"Fine. You may continue."

"He had slowed to idle and shifted into reverse (they were going with the current, remember), jockeying the cruiser back and forth, keeping her in line with the harbor buoy (a flashing green light floating thirty feet to his left) and then gradually inching back until the bow (actually, the anchor) was more or less abeam of the buoy, where he held her, stalled, hanging in the current until 11:05, when he gave one blast on the horn—the signal for Ali to release the windlass brake."

\*

. . . Once away, the sixty-pound anchor shot straight down: chain pouring after it through the hawse pipe, paying out with a chatter as it reeved cleanly over the wildcat. The Danforth hit hard, its long tapered flukes biting deep and then taking hold as the cruiser reversed slowly, dragging the blades under to their shank while yellow chain spilled along the bottom in an ever-lengthening southward course, falling through the inky water with a serpentine motion, clanking down and piling up in heaps . . .

\*

"By then the river had reversed, so he cut the engines and let the new current back the boat until she was fast."

"How long did this take?"

" A minute, maybe more."

"Which means that the divers now had less than forty-five minutes remaining."

"Yes, but don't forget—they had been rehearsing this operation, both in and out of the water, for nearly a month."

"That being the case, what went wrong?"

"Accidents happen," George said philosophically.

\*

. . . The scarred man set the minute hand on his diving watch at zero and then dropped backwards off the swimstep, landing on his tanks and rolling as he sank, righting himself effortlessly in that dark and weightless world that closed over him like sleep until he switched on the underwater lamp, holding it ahead in one hand as he dipped under the rudder and passed beneath the keel and then dove, driving with his flippers down to the anchor line, where he swung round, clinging by his free hand, to wait for the others.

The swaying chain gave off an eerie greenish-yellow glow, slanting down sharply and tapering off to a thread before it vanished into deep darkness. He listened to the hubbly-bubbly of his breathing and the creaking of the hull, watching them come, in succession, gliding over to him lamp by lamp.

Then he turned on his head lamp and pushed off, going down with the group trailing in single file (Ahmed; Moussa swimming with the boring tool held crosswise like a trapeze; Mohammed bringing up the rear with a lamp in one hand and a short phosphorescent grapnel in the other), feeling himself grow heavier as he descended (the rising pressure squeezing his mangled ear with a vengeance), following the J-like sag of the chain to a depth of fifty-six feet before it curled under and flattened out to slope gradually toward the bottom (less than fifteen feet below him now), where in the playing lamplight he saw clumps of dark vegetation waving their tendrils like huge overturned beetles and quick puffs of sediment from creatures scuttling off into the gloom.

He looked back once to count the lamps. Facing forward again, he found himself within inches of a school of large silvery perch: staring at him with alarmed bulging eyes and coming straight on so that he had no time to react before they divided, parting into planes of glittering tinsel that exploded over and around him, under his outstretched arms, streaking past his face mask—the entire shimmering mass spurting out of sight without a sound and disappearing in a shower of sparkles beyond which, rising from the bottom like a mound of yellow coral, he saw the end of the chain.

The anchor lay buried at sixty-eight feet. Regrouping above it, they fanned out toward the Jersey bank and almost immediately sighted the cage—a dullyellow reflection twenty feet away, resting just downstream from the channel buoy's sinker block.

The scarred man checked his watch: four minutes had elapsed. . . .

\*

"What was that stuff he painted on my forehead?"

"A chemical solution possessing certain anodic properties."

George stared at him. "What the hell does *that* mean?"

"A conductor. Its effectiveness, you should bear in mind on your return to the subject, remains intact for several hours. What happened next?"

\*

. . . They separated: Moussa and Mohammed swerving right to head for the sinker block; Ahmed and the scarred man settling down beside the cage—the latter wielding both lamps while Ahmed dropped the cage side door and removed the canvas-covered charge, slipping one arm through the thick coil of detonating cable as he eased it out.

By then Moussa, first laying his lamp and the boring tool on top of the barnacled sinker, had turned on the floodlight waiting for Mohammed to cross the twelve feet to the target and signify its position by waving his lamp. He then loosened the oversized set screws on the steel frame connecting the light to its battery box, centered the halo on Mohammed, then tightened the screws, collected his equipment, and kicked off for the target. . . .

\*

"How did they weigh that light down?"

"They didn't. They drilled holes in the concrete ledge and bolted on a steel plate to which they welded a metal frame (something on the order of a box, open at the top to allow for changing the batteries), fitted with screw holes aligned with those on the lamp frame to enable them to lock the beam in place.''

"Welding, yet. Your Abdul left very little to chance.''

"He made them spend two weeks alone staking out the outside edge of the tube—sending them down day and night: starting from a point downriver and working slowly up with the metal detectors, placing the bars at intervals of ten to fifteen feet—setting up an infallible east-west line on both sides of the river (roping things off, you might say), planting the bars right up to the sinker blocks; and then going back to the beginning: making a duplicate "run" with the detectors to verify the placement of each bar—that's how little he left to chance. The rest was easy: all they had to do was move in fourteen feet north and establish the target sites, as close as possible to the sinker blocks in order to best utilize those big lights.''

"Speaking of which: a while ago you mentioned glare," the Interrogator prompted.

"Diffraction, due to the amount of sediment in suspension. Water, especially dirty water, tends to reflect light in all directions.''

"Therefore?''

"Tinted glass in their face masks.''

"How did they mark this target?''

"A bar driven a measured four and one-half feet into the mud.''

"Four and one-half feet being?''

"The maximum depth of the silt at that point, based on sonar readings Abdul had taken in early October.''

*

. . . Seven minutes had gone by before Mohammed sank the grapnel to its ring and unwound the short attached rope and slipped his flipper through the loop, drawing it snug around his ankle. Standing, he took the extra tank from Moussa and faced south with his back to the current (as yet a soft insistent nudging he had only to lean against to offset), pressing the butt-end to his

chest and vising both arms along the cylinder. He waited until
Moussa, behind him now, gripped him around the waist and
then, aiming the conical nozzle at the target, he thumbed open
the valve. . . .

*

"Full blast?"

"Hell, no. That air was under twenty-five hundred pounds of
compression per square inch. If he had opened it all the way, the
tank would have taken off like a Poseidon missile. There was an
adjustable governor on the regulator. Abdul had made him practice
over and over (dress rehearsals, excavating smaller trenches) to
determine the highest volume he could safely control. Even so, the
blast carried him back and up, dragging Moussa along, until the
rope stiffened, at which point he cut off the air and floated down
and waited for the current to clear away the debris. Then he aimed
the nozzle in a new direction and repeated the procedure: working
from side to side, carving out a long oval depression."

"And how much time did these hydro-gymnastics consume?"

"The tank's audio-reserve bell had been set to sound automati-
cally at the end of thirteen minutes. That was Moussa's cue to start
digging with the boring tool."

"The other two divers—what were they up to during this ac-
robatic interlude?"

"They had to peel the canvas off and prepare the charge. Don't
ask me how; I only know that it was complicated business: working
behind the light on that ledge, one holding a lamp and trying to
balance more than four feet of high explosive while the other did
whatever it was he had to do in (at best) shadowy light. The fact
that the current was getting stronger didn't help matters any."

*

. . . Minus twenty-two minutes:

On their way across to the target (each supporting an end of
the bright-orange, bullet-shaped charge) Ahmed and the scarred

man swam into a cross-current eddy that swept by them in one long eastward-rolling billow, lifting them sharply and nearly shaking the charge loose before it surged on. Both men exchanged looks before proceeding over to where Moussa hunched in the basin, with the boring tool, leaning hard on the handles, enveloped to the waist in filmy particles churned up by the whirling blades. He jammed the shaft back and forth, prying up chunks of mud and clay, and then stepped back to scrape the blades while Mohammed bent down in the roily cloud to toss the clods out of the trench. . . .

\*

"This chamber."

"Round," George said, "close to three feet in circumference—the idea being to leave twelve inches of clearance for the bomb. As they went deeper, Moussa hung over so far into the opening that Ahmed had to hold him up by the weight belt. Toward the end Mohammed was disappearing completely into the hole. The rim was chin-high when he struck gold." He hesitated. "Oil, if you prefer."

\*

. . . When it happened, Mohammed sprang halfway out of the hole, waving excitedly to the others. He dropped to his knees once more to make certain, and then bounded up again, drumming on the rim as though it were an imaginary tom-tom.

The scarred man made a thumbs-up sign and then beckoned him out, pointing to his watch. They had exactly eleven minutes left . . .

\*

The interrogator wore a doubtful expression. "Vibrations?"

"Strong, too. Throbbing six feet below them. Undeniable proof that they had scored a bull's-eye."

"One moment. They had used up thirteen minutes removing

five and one-half feet of mud. I take it the next step was to bury the bomb. How, then, did they negotiate that additional six feet with only ten minutes remaining?''

"By applying Newton's second law of motion," George said smugly. "Moussa and Mohammed forced the charge down manually as far as they could—I would guess a foot or so. The top had been converted to a circular steel housing for the base of that modified tank with the conical nozzle. Somehow (and again, I don't have the foggiest) they locked the two together. Then they simply pointed the nozzle straight up and opened the valve. The pressure drove the charge out of sight in less than two minutes.''

"Clever," the Interrogator conceded.

*

. . . Navigating by his head lamp and paying out detonating cable as he went, the scarred man swam over to the sinker block and waited for Ahmed—who came behind planing low above the bottom with his left hand on the cable, pausing every few feet to remove a long barbed u-bolt from the scabbard on his thigh and staple the cable to the riverbed.

They began the slow ascent up the buoy chain together: the scarred man in the lead—still paying out cable and stopping every twenty feet to press the exhaust button on his chest to keep his suit from swelling as the air inside expended; while below him Ahmed fell rapidly behind: halting repeatedly to twine his legs around the chain and crank a length of wire out of a yellow pannier on his weight belt, snipping it off with a large pair of yellow cutters hanging beside the pannier and then tying the detonating cable to the chain—his progress so hampered by the stepped-up current and the undulating chain that by the time he reached the surface the scarred man was sitting in the dinghy with Ali. . . .

*

"The explosive had to penetrate eighteen inches of concrete and five inches of steel," George summarized.

"Also, that intervening eighteen inches of mud," the Interrogator said, "—the charge itself being fifty-four inches long."

"And capable of blasting a hole thirty-six inches in circumference and twelve feet deep through solid reinforced concrete," George amended. "Abdul estimated that it would burn through the tunnel roof in four-tenths of a second."

*

. . . Ahmed clung to the prow of the dinghy, treading water while the scarred man leaned over the gunnel and inserted the bulb-like receiver into a socket drilled into the buoy's metal crown and then passed him the coil of detonating cable. He lashed the surplus to the bottom of the buoy, leaving ten feet of slack to account for the tides. They were pulling him into the boat when a dark object broke water nearby with a swoosh. It bobbed on the current, looking like a giant bloated frog floating on its back. . . .

*

"Contributing factors?" George mused. "Well, the river was stronger than Abdul had anticipated, particularly the cross-currents. Also, Moussa ran out of air—most likely a result of his exertions on the boring tool. His audio-reserve bell went off while he was helping Mohammed unlock the tank from that housing. He had two minutes of air left, and no alternative but to surface. Besides, save collecting the tools and depositing them in the cage, they were done. Mohammed indicated that he had everything under control. So Moussa waved goodbye and set out for the anchor chain."

"The question still obtains—what went wrong?"

"We'll never know," George confessed. "Moussa didn't look back."

*

. . . Had he looked back he would have seen Mohammed

shoulder the boring tool over to the cage (struggling to maneuver in the now half-knot current bearing down on him in its
rush to the sea like a cold hard wind); would have seen him fight
his way back to the target and retrieve the tank; and an instant
later would have seen the eddy spin out of the blackness beyond
the target in one high whirling mass that kicked up sewage and
sediment in a wide eastward path, rippling the halo of light into
a network of wavy lines and slamming into Mohammed just
before he reached the sinker block; would have seen him
catapult against the buoy chain—he grabbing it instinctively
with his free hand and managing to twist one leg around for
leverage and hang on, still holding tight to the tank, it banging
on the ledge while he rode the eddy out and then dropped down
beside the light, steadying the butt-end of the tank with one
hand, failing to notice the thin bead of bubbles escaping from
the nozzle. Bending over, he lifted the base in both hands to
draw it to him just as the safety valve exploded with a sharp
ping, propelling the tank forward like a shot to strike him in the
right temple, snapping his head over and sending him reeling
backwards, kicking clumsily as he rose, his body shuddering,
the head flopping as he went up—slowly at first and then
accelerating rapidly as his suit ballooned. . . .

*

"They buried him at sea on the eighteenth," said George.

"Touching. Why the delay?"

"They couldn't just toss him overboard. It had to be done some
distance out to sea, which meant time—and time was scarce;
remember, there was still the New York side to mine. They spent
all day the seventeenth cleaning their equipment, refilling the
tanks—putting everything in order for that evening."

"Who took his place?"

"Abdul—who else?" George said. "There were no accidents
this time—they had an hour and eleven minutes of workable slack
water on the seventeenth." He yawned. "Are we finished?"

The Interrogator's smile was reassuring. "Almost. We haven't
covered the detonation system yet."

"There isn't much to cover. Two high-frequency receivers, each about the size of a golf ball with spiraled seams of tinfoil coated with clear shellac for an antenna, and a tiny battery inside. The transmitter was one of those little remote control devices used to pilot model planes, except that instead of two joy sticks it had a control button and a range of five miles. All Abdul needed to do was position the cruiser in a direct line of sight between the two buoys and then push the button when Ali gave him the word over the walkie-talkie."

"One more item," the Interrogator promised, "Why Abdul?"

"Talk to the Committee—they gave the order," George said.

"Surely you must have some idea as to their motive. Was it the money?"

George shut his eyes; said "Only in part," in a tired voice before opening them. "And not the money so much as the ultimatum that came with it. For that matter, the ultimatum merely confirmed the verdict they had reached initially in August after deciding to go ahead with the tunnel. They really had no choice about Abdul. In the final analysis, his value derived from his invisibility, that extraordinary mobility his cover afforded him. From this standpoint he was the perfect agent. Once the tunnel exploded, however, he would have been a marked man. Sooner or later, someone would have gotten to him—if not your secret service, then the CIA; and he knew too much for the Committee to risk that."

"The *fedayeen* were aware of this from the start?"

"I briefed them myself. We had our plan, too, you see."

"Which called for him and the boy to become . . . romantically involved," the Interrogator concluded.

George said bluntly, "One of Ali's tasks was to take it in the ass. We had to provide Abdul with some distraction, keep him occupied from time to time, get him off the boat occasionally so the *fedayeen* could assemble the bomb and run the detonating wire from the engine room to the prow—drilling holes in the paneling and pulling it up the wall cavity and across the ceiling and through the bulkheads and under the forward deck (stringing a few feet every chance they got, then hiding their tracks with wood filler and varnish and paint) until they guided it to one of those vertical chrome rods on the bowsprit rail. The rod was hollow anyway; all they did was saw off the tip and attach the wire to the receiver, which they clamped to the top of the rod.''

"They stuck the receiver in plain view?"

"Not until the eighteenth.''

The Interrogator saw the connection—"During Mohammed's funeral services.''

"While they were weighting his body down with the air compressor,'' George specified. "Abdul had gone below, refusing as usual to have anything to do with their prayers. Wrapped in tinfoil, the receiver was indistinguishable from a distance—the same color as chrome in the sunlight. And Abdul was occupied on the bridge for the rest of the afternoon: going up and down the river, keeping to the same pattern he had been following for weeks. Even if he climbed down to the bow in the final minutes, the odds were that he would not come close to the bowsprit, and that if he did, his attention would be concentrated on the buoys and the river.''

"Ali detonated the bomb, then?"

George grinned. "They tuned their receiver to the same frequency as the other two on the buoys, the only difference being that it operated on a time-delay of fifteen seconds.''

"He blew him*self* up?"

George widened the grin—"A fitting end for a man of many parts, eh?''

# Old Wounds
# and Other Injuries

*Le Bourget lies on the northeast side of Paris. Once a major commercial air strip (indeed, the very landing field where Charles Lindbergh ended his historic flight in 1927), it is now restricted mainly to private aircraft—such as the blue sixteen-passanger Learjet warming up beside the Rothschild hangar at 8:00 New York time on October 18th.*

*A silver Bentley drew up beside the Lear at 8:04, the chauffeur seeming to emerge from the car at the exact moment that the wheels came to a stop. He opened the back door on the driver's side and stood smartly at attention while the two men got out and walked over to the plane. They exchanged a few words, shook hands, the old nobleman (a tall graceful figure wearing a Homburg) patting the General's shoulder before they parted. The General waved once as the Bentley drove off; then he climbed into the cabin.*

*The pilot came aft five minutes after they had taken off. He was a slightly built, competent-looking little man with a surprisingly deep voice. "Our flying time will be approximately eight hours, mon Général. We may encounter some headwind turbulence over the mid-Atlantic, but otherwise it should be a comfortable trip. I regret that we must do without the services of our regular cabin crew, but the chef has left his compliments in the form of two precooked, four-course meals. Can I get you anything?"*

*"A glass of orange juice, perhaps," the General said, removing the tape recorder from his briefcase. He waited for the pilot to pull the table-top down from a wall panel, then popped a cassette into*

*the recorder and said: "I may eat something later. Right now, though, I would like to work."*

*"Very good, mon Général."*

*The General tore off the end of an unopened envelope that had reached him in Paris the day before. He shook out two sheets of paper, one a note from his secretary that read:*

*Darling,*

*Here is the information you requested from Sydney. Am I crazy, or did they send us the wrong page? I can't make head nor tuschie of it.*

*Oh—try to finish the account of your wound if possible. The publisher wants to wrap up Volume One posthaste.*

*I miss you.*

*Mollie*

*He read the other sheet of paper twice (grunting with amusement several times), then snapped the recorder going:*

*Very well, Mollie my own, we will finish the story today. The real story—not the bullshit my biographers invented, nor the fable taught as history to Israeli schoolchildren. This, my love, is the unexpurgated truth. . . .*

*To begin, I quote from paragraph two, page 187 of* The Australian War Annals. 1939–1945:

". . . Having made its way north along the coastal road, the 473rd Detachment came under heavy fire shortly after 7 A.M. as they approached a stone emplacement on the outskirts of Iskanderun. The Australians stormed the position and took it, afterwards laying siege to the nearby fort. A fierce battle ensued, with French reinforcements attacking from an orchard close to the road. Some of Sergeant Wiggins' men routed this advance, killing two of the enemy and capturing a mortar. Seizing the initiative, Sergeant Wiggins then personally knocked out a machine-gun emplacement with hand grenades and although wounded led his men in an all-out assault. During the taking of the fort, one of the Jewish guides was wounded. . . .''

(*Laughs*)

\*

I feared as much. The redoubtable Sergeant Wiggins, that dear old anti-Semitic digger, sent in his hagiography instead of a battle report. No mention of Joseph . . . nor of that magnificent half-naked Senegalese and his machete act.

Nor of the fact that it was dark and we were in a half-track going north down a rutted dirt road with the sea on our left. I sat next to the open cab holding my knees fetus-fashion, caught in the grip of a profound, almost sexual thrill. Chest-tight, dry-mouthed anticipation. Rather like watching one's woman undress for the first time.

1941—Good God, I was twenty-six years old. Had all my hair and most of my illusions, both sparse now. Quite the romantic: wanting to prove myself, seeing war as the supreme rite of passage, a test I dare not fail. Waiting semi-erect with all my senses alive and raw in the chilly sea-scented morning air on the day the British invaded Vichy Syria.

There were two guides, actually: myself and Joseph Bloch. Got up like Arabs: wearing burnooses over our JSP uniforms because Haganah had contracted to supply the British Army with Arabic-speaking personnel for work behind the lines. An admirable scheme, whereby we gained much needed military seasoning; but a frail umbilical as contracts went—seeing that the French shot captured Jews as spies or else handed them over to their Arab allies, who performed their traditional amputations, the most common being what we in Haganah referred to as terminal circumcision.

We had been assigned (Joseph since he knew the way; I because Ben Gurion wanted me to learn the ropes)—assigned to conduct seventeen Australian infantrymen (one of whom, predictably, was Irish) to a bridge outside Iskanderun. Said structure to be taken and held pending the appearance of Third Armor Group at dawn.

The brakes squealed suddenly, then locked, and the half-track clanked to a stop in a cloud of powdery dust. We piled out and moved off the road while the driver turned around, pausing long enough to toss a jaunty salute and call out "Jolly good hunting, you chaps!" before the caterpillar treads threw up a smokescreen as he roared back toward Palestine.

"Cheerful bloke, ain't 'e?" someone remarked.

"Aye, and well out of it, the lucky devil," said another.

(Yegods, Mollie, Australian dialect. Mongrelized as Cockney: $a$'s turned into $i$'s; $e$'s in place of $a$'s; the same profusion of faintly Oriental diphthongs. Naturally they looked askance upon my in-those-days carefully polished British accent.)

Forming a column, we set out northeast across a series of low sandy hills dotted with thorn bushes and sharp rocks. The morning was windless, brilliantly lit by intense starlight. In the east a pearlwhite moon floated serene above black mountain humps. After a bit the land warped upward, lost its sandy character. Cultivated fields appeared. We were resting in a grove of stunted olive trees when an explosion whumped in the distance like thunder. An orange ball of flame, perhaps five kilometers away, rose in the south.

"What d'you make of it?" asked a youthful voice.

"The 'aff-track," someone answered in a dead undertone. "They've cut the bloody road."

"Maybe the Tommy . . ." the youthful voice began, fading as the rapid putputput of submachine gun fire reached our ears.

We filed out of the grove in silence. The driver, like most of the Aussies, had been armed with a bolt-action Lee Enfield, and there was nothing more to say.

Two hours later we topped a ridge and looked down on the sleeping village of Iskanderun. It was four o'clock, so still you could hear the sea crashing against the nearby cliffs.

Iskanderun. Surrounded by a thick white rectangular wall within which the closely packed walled mud houses resembled an asymmetrical network of honeycombs sprawling across a fairly level plateau, its western edge jutting out over the sea. To the north, extensive orange groves. Row after row of date palms on the eastern fringe. A typical Arab town: ancient and dirty and small, unchanged in its essentials since the time of Vespasian—who probably rode past it on his way to sack Jerusalem.


Which reminds me, Mollie, if you'll pardon a brief digression:

I drove past it (like Vespasian, although going in the opposite direction) on my way to sack a *Fatah* stronghold in 1957. Stopped off on the return to make a pilgrimage (my first and last) to the shrine of my mutilation—which had been transformed into a combination post office-schoolhouse for an Israeli settlement founded less than a year earlier. Paid a visit afterwards to the deserted village. Oranges and dates and olives still flourished, but Iskanderun had disappeared under bombs and napalm in the 1956 War. What remained after the air strike bulldozers had reduced to rubble. (In keeping with Ben Gurion's dictum that the best way to insure that villagers will not return is to remove the village.)

I came upon a Bedouin family camped beneath one of the few walls still standing. Several children squatted in a rocky courtyard giving me the once-over. Boggled by my patch. One finally walked over to me, curiosity overcoming his reticence. Had a stick tied to his wrist with a piece of string. The string in turn was tied to a worm that lived in the child's body.

*Dracunculus medinensis.*

The Guinea worm. Thread-thin, the oldest-known parasite of man. Excluding *Homo sapiens* himself.

By turning the stick slowly, not unlike reeling in a kite, they simply roll the bugger out. The trick being timing: waiting until the worm has attained the proper size and then taking care not to pull it apart, which causes blood poisoning. The female of the species has been known to reach a length of three feet.

An antediluvian remedy, this tethering procedure. Quite common in Europe during the Middle Ages, it can be traced back to the days of Moses.

The boy was big-bellied, runty. Large grave eyes, as black as his future. He lifted the string a fraction, his face lighting up as the thing slithered from its hole looking like a filament of hair coated with snot, the tip wiggling with a minute disgusting motion. Offered to let me touch it; wanted me to remove my eye patch in exchange. Tit for tat. I declined on both counts.

Browned off, he was. Retreated to a safe distance and chased me away with rocks and insults, tossing both with Bedouin accuracy. To the delight of the women and a gnarled old grandfather clad in black who followed me with red-rimmed hate-filled eyes.

I drove across the bridge and left the orderly to guard the jeep while I went up into the hills. Climbed to the spot where we had lain on that morning long ago when Iskanderun, asleep on its ledge by the starry sea, had suggested an Arcadian peacefulness.

*

But getting back to 1941:

Directly below us a tidal inlet cut transversely across the plateau, winding east through a deep gorge. An old-fashioned metal bridge spanned the gap, its single-truss support beams rising to a dark triangular point in the moonlight. A figure leaned against the railing at the far end.

Moving back from the ridge, we dropped down amidst a small outcrop of boulders. Sergeant Wiggins crouched in front of us, braced against his Tommy gun.

Wiggins. My nemesis, if ever one I had. A burly, pugnosed man with squinty blue eyes. One of those gruff redheaded Australians who always seem on the verge of losing their tempers.

He had ignored me completely until then, confining himself to grunts whenever communication with Joseph was unavoidable. I saw nothing peculiar in this; on the contrary, it seemed a suitable deportment for the kind of fire-eating taciturn commando I imagined him to be—saving his energy, his very breath, for the real thing. The aloof manner and brooding silence of the others I interpreted as the unmistakable hallmark of hand-picked battle-savvy veterans who preferred to keep their distance from such rank amateurs as Joseph and myself. That they might not relish the presence of Jews never dawned on me, of course.

Even when Wiggins said, "We sit tight for a spell, lads," I was not disabused. Clearly, he wanted to give us a chance to catch our wind, cagey tactician that he was.

Yet I wished to make a good impression—that of the unblooded novice eager as a colt to spring from the trenches of his inexperience, leading a charge over the top in search of deeds worthy to be sung by a scop. So I stated forthrightly that I disapproved of waiting.

(Wagging my tongue with less thought than a dog shaking its tail. Tact never my forte—what little I possessed inherited from a father who'd had almost none to spare. No one ever needed to ask for his opinion, either.)

Wiggins glanced at me without shifting his weight. There came a pregnant pause, during which he commenced to scratch his genitals. Then he said: "When I want advice from an effing Yid, Moses, I'll letcha know."

Using Moses in the collective sense, you see; rhyming the first syllable with that in Mao Tse-tung. *Maoses.*

Soft tittering from several of the lads.

Until, mercifully, an Irish voice checked in with: "Maybe he's right, top. Maybe we *should* have a go at it now."

Lavery by name. Tall and rubbery, fitted with a long comical face and a nose you could hang a hat on.

Wiggins waxed indignant: "Are you round the bloody bend? One shot we'd 'ave Frenchies and wogs down around our ears."

"Shooting ain't the only means of disposal," Lavery advanced.

"Leave it, mate," Wiggins told him. "If the road's been sliced, Third effing Armor will be a bit delayed, now won't they? Might not even get through, right? So we'd be risking our necks for nothing. Something else you ain't thought of neither: if the Frenchies 'ave the road they know we're 'ere. Seen us go by; counted us, likely. Which means when that demo crew returns, yon sentry will be getting some additional aid. They'll be ex*pect*ing us, sport."

"*If* it's been cut," Lavery said.

"Leave it," Wiggins repeated.

"Like hell I will," Lavery said. "What if that was only a wog raiding party what done the Tommy? I say we takes our chances with one Frenchie while we've got him, by God, instead of strumming our clackers until a bloody platoon shows up."

Wiggins stood in a huff. "And *I* say we picks our noses for an hour, Irish. Nothing 'appens by then, we'll see about the ruddy bridge." So having spake, the knight of the unfortunate face, still clawing at his privates, ambled off to keep an eye on the sentry.

And an hour later dropped the bomb—coming up to Joseph with a disarming smile to explain: "One of you two mates will 'ave to do the sentry, Moses." Held out his bayonet, said reasonably: "I can't expose my lads; 'e'd open fire soon as 'e spotted the uni."

Joseph, who spoke four languages and a half-dozen Arab dialects but whose English was rudimentary, fired "He says?" to me in Hebrew.

I imparted Wiggins' master plan.

Staring at the bayonet as though it were a scorpion, Joseph backed up a step. "All they told me to do was find the bridge," he said incredulously.

"Cut the wog-talk," Wiggins ordered. "We're all white 'ere. What's the matter, sport?" he inquired of Joseph. "Knees a bit wonky?" Turned to me, said: "I thought you Jews was keen for action awhile ago." Extending the bayonet.

"Tell the idiot to stuff it," said Joseph.

*

You would have liked Joseph, Mollie. He was eighteen years old, good as only the young are good. He had been a prodigy, having published his first article on archaeology (written in French, printed in a Paris journal) at the age of sixteen. His passion for the past had led him on solitary and quite dangerous expeditions across a third of southern Syria: dressed like a Bedouin, picking up dialects like shells on a beach—exploits which had brought him to the attention of Haganah, who tapped his knowledge of enemy terrain and found therein a vast reservoir of strategic information.

A noncombatant, he had agreed to guide the Aussies simply because it was a new adventure.

Several months after the adventure, upon my release from Hadassah Hospital, I went to his house in Jerusalem. There were pictures of Joseph, an only child, on every wall. His father, a modest man who taught Hebrew grammar at the Popular University, welcomed me politely. Served me tea, averting his eyes from my face—this was before my plastic surgery.

Professor Bloch apologized for his wife's absence: she had been having a rough time. He had no sooner tendered the apology than Joseph's mother entered the room.

Walking heavily, a large woman with sunken cheeks and unkempt gray hair. She wore a baggy sweater over a rumpled blue dress, both of which had obviously been slept in. Stood hesitant, her eyes moving around the room as though seeing it for the first time.

Professor Bloch gave her an anxious look and started to rise.

"Sit," she said in a tired voice, waving him off. "I promise not to be difficult."

She plopped down in a rocker, ran a hand through her hair, said (to no one, to the room itself): "They would not open Joseph's coffin. I begged them, but they refused." Fingered a button on the sweater, twisting it absentmindedly as she asked: "Were you with him . . . when . . ."—making a helpless gesture with her hand to supply the words she could not speak.

"I was not far away," I said. An equivocation, but technically true.

Her next words were addressed to the floor: "Did he suffer greatly?"

"No," I lied.

She nodded to herself, swallowing hard. Finally looked at my face, her eyes (puffy, absolutely lost) registering first shock, then pity. "Forgive me," she said, "I did not mean to seem insensitive. Tell your mother that I share in her sorrow."

And without thinking, like a fool I said: "She is dead."

"*Ach*," she groaned, turning away. Hugging herself. Began

rocking, asked the ceiling: "And for what? To help the English murder the French. The latest installment in that glorious Zionist plan to build a Jewish *wehrmacht* so that Weizmann and his pack of fanatics can steal Palestine from the Arabs. Dear God, what insanity."

"Gerda," Professor Bloch said softly.

But she could not stop. "We left Germany for Joseph's sake," she confided to the wall. "I did not understand his gifts, but it was plain that any boy who could teach himself Aramaic at the age of twelve had some that were formidable. Our problem was finding a place where he would have the opportunity to develop them. Because things were bad, you cannot imagine, by 1936—even in little Marburg. I have never seen such hatred as that on the faces of the crowd who cheered, goaded by a professor from my husband's own department, as the Brown Shirts burned the *heder*. It was terrifying. Most of them, you see, were people we had lived among all our lives. Suddenly, almost overnight it seemed, they had become not just strangers, but enemies. You could smell the pogrom coming like the odor of rain. So we sold everything, *gave* our home away to a German *schadenfroher* who would have made a pawnbroker blush for shame, and came to Palestine, where Noah would be able to teach and Joseph would be safe." She wrung her nose with a kerchief, then added bitterly: "*Safe*. With Arabs and Jews living apart, each in their own ghetto, a wall of mistrust and ignorance in between. Hating each other for the best of reasons. No mutual respect, no love or understanding . . . My God, we came here to *escape* bigotry . . . only to find this Ben Gurion ranting like a Nazi on a street corner . . ."

". . . Dear," Professor Bloch pleaded from the edge of his seat.

She closed her eyes and nodded. "Forgive me," she said. "I have become a little mad."

*

"Have you gone crazy?" was Joseph's reaction when I took the bayonet from Wiggins' outstretched hand.

Who clapped me on the shoulder and said "Give 'im the wog routine until you're close enough, Moses, and then polish 'im off." Jerking a clenched fist across his throat to illustrate: "Like the Gurkhas."

I doubled back, worked my way down to the road, and crawled along the hilly eastern shoulder until it leveled off, leaving fifty yards of flat ground between me and the bridge, which stood off to my right at the end of a crescent-shaped curve. Tucked the bayonet in my sash next to my revolver, stepped out and started walking with a shuffling Arab gait.

Assuming he would challenge me at once, of course.

Unfortunately, ten long seconds went by without a peep from him. Hadn't moved, in fact. Still resting on the railing. I wondered was he dozing? And if so, how the blazes should one get his attention? For one had no desire (given the shattering possibilities of a flustered corporal with a rifle in his hands) to bounce onto the bridge unannounced.

In a trice came the solution: a *deus ex machina* in the form of a rock that spilled me flat on my face. Rolled down an embankment. Got up spitting dust and snorting blood, ululating like a ruptured baboon.

Un-Gurkhaesque, to be sure; but on the other hand, I felt reasonably certain that I had captured his attention.

Felt certain also that I had broken my nose.

And lost a large chunk of the initiative.

Along with, alas, both bayonet and revolver.

And him as well: girders now blocking the spot where he had been standing. Unless, it struck me with heartsinking force, for some reason he had moved. Dropped to his knees, say.

And all at once the moonlight seemed unbearably bright.

Next, as I recall, I shot my hands into the air and shouted: *"Aime! Aime arabe!"* as I galloped, fearing he would be the sort who'd shoot first and save the *interrogatoire* for later; and then suddenly out of nowhere *"Cessez le feu!"* popped into my head and tumbled from my mouth; and thusly: alternately *"Aime arabe!"* with *"Cessez le feu!"* praying my atrocious pronunciation might sound a note of authenticity, convince the sentry that, as I most fervently proclaimed, I was nothing more than a friendly Arab who asked only that he cease firing—in this fashion I went clattering onto the wooden flooring, where I froze.

Having seen him by then. My mouth fell open.

As, in a voice full of phlegm and irritation and contempt, speaking in rich old Arabic, he said: "In the name of Allah, what manner of jackassedness art thou up to, and what is that gibberish thou art braying in the dead of night?"

Lo and behold: an old Syrian waiting for the early bus to Beirut.

We tied him up and put him under the bridge.

Lavery, who bound his hands, said: "Gob, if we'd held off another hour, he'd've died of old age."

"*Mar*velous demonstration of footwork, Moses," Wiggins complimented me. "I'm surprised 'e didn't laugh 'imself to death."

"*Cessez le feu?*" was Joseph's terse evaluation of the whole disgraceful affair.

*

One more digression, Mollie—another item for the file on Gerda Bloch: who crossed my path again in . . . 1951? No, 1952.

She rang me up while I was on leave in Jerusalem celebrating my promotion to major general. Her voice was unfamiliar: loud and friendly and grating, coming over the wire like a hearty rasp interrupted at intervals by a bad connection that made words crackle like popcorn. She said it had been a long time, and I agreed; wanted to see me: an offer of tea and chat. I hemmed and hawed but finally accepted, out of curiosity more than anything else.

For she was at the height of her fame and unpopularity by then—having devoted the intervening eleven years to organizing a left-wing party that campaigned for Palestinian rights. (Even in those halcyon days an undertaking equivalent to launching a drive for the care and feeding of lions among Christian slaves in the

Colosseum.) She edited the party newspaper as well. And wrote books—her latest an embarrassingly well-documented *cause célèbre* which described the Zionist movement as a product of colonialist mentality. Having in short made of herself an all-round pain in the ear for the Israeli Establishment.

Having also, on the death of Professor Bloch in 1950, become a widow.

I found her in a tiny office proofing copy under a plastic eyeshade. Looking surprisingly chipper. No longer heavy—gaunt now, and grayer, but with fire in her eyes. Greeted me gaily with: "Welcome to the queen of the lunatic fringe"—an allusion to Golda Meir's most recent broadside.

She chainsmoked her way through two cups of tea while we made small talk; was puffing her fifth Lucky Strike when I mentioned in passing that the Prime Minister was in a stew over her last editorial. "He fears you may force him to close the paper under the Sedition Act," I warned her.

"I preach facts, not insurrection," she told me curtly. "Your friend Ben Gurion fears the truth."

I said that calling Israel a racist society was stretching it a bit.

"Five hundred thousand Palestinians live in this country," she replied. "They make up at least one-third of the population. And yet the only Arabs permitted in the Knesset are janitors."

I countered with an observation borrowed from Ben Gurion: "To share the benefits of citizenship, they must first demonstrate a willingness to accept its liabilities. Under the circumstances, faith and trust cannot be given, they must be earned."

Which earned me a withering look. "How well you ape the master," she said. "We stand knee-deep in moral quicksand and he throws out platitudes instead of rope."

I poured us another cup of tea, she needing both hands and all ten fingers to tick off a tirade that went something like this: "No unions. Even though they comprise fifty percent of our work force—ninety percent of our unskilled labor. They empty our garbage cans and clean our sewers and trim our hedges, maintain our roads, grind our grain, mix our cement—all without the benefits and protection a union affords even the lowliest Jewish shoemaker. That cow Meir loves to moo about the Zionist fortress her crowd is building, but she neglects to acknowledge who the hod carriers are. No real education. We shove them into ghettos, spend one-tenth of the amount on their schools that we allocate to our own. The result, in terms of elementary and secondary training, is a cruel joke. The only adequate institutions available to them are vocational—*these* we support wholeheartedly: supplying the lathes and presses and saws, insuring that no Arab boy lacks for hammer and nails (by then, of course, the girls have traded in their textbooks for a broom and bowl while we look the other way); because we do not want them to compete with *our* children by producing doctors or lawyers or architects or thinkers or writers; because we do not want any intellectuals crawling out of the garbage pile to complain about the smell, no shapers who have the audacity to want a hand in planning their own destiny; no—we offer them *en masse* the same future Mississippi parcels out to her Negroes: the heady promise of one day being able to assemble a carburetor. And when by chance we are confronted with that rare phoenix who by some miracle has managed to escape this psychic dungeon with his or her brains unimpaired, we use every bureaucratic trick in the book to deny them entrance to our universities. Housing, employment, medical aid, you name it—in no area do they have parity with Jews. So don't quote me any cocktail-party cant about the liabilities of citizenship. And keep that mumbo jumbo about faith and trust under your helmet. We confiscate their property without paying for it; reserve the right to search their homes without warrant; subject them to being shaken down in public at the whim of a traffic policeman; deport those who dare speak out: without trial, spiriting them across the border as Herzl recommended—if anyone has the right to demand a show of confidence, it is *them*, not us." And so on in this vein until both she and her tea cooled down.

But enough of Gerda Bloch, Mollie—back to the tale of the missing eye.

*

Not even the promise of dawn gave me any solace after my debacle on the bridge. The Aussies, by contrast, were drowning themselves in comfort with a half-dozen bottles of *arak* pinched from the old Syrian's bag.

Wiggins ushered in the day by crawling off to do a grunting noisy rear into the gorge.

Lavery unwound from sleep like a spider and went topside to piss from the bridge. We heard him walk across, return twenty minutes later, call down: "Looks like the war's over, top—leastways for us. Ain't no armor coming down that road."

Belting his breeches, Wiggins cleared his nose and throat; hawked several oyster-sized gobs; scratched head, belly, and those verminous balls; then lifted his bleary eyes to Lavery and gargled: "Right. Probably gave us up when the 'aff-track didn't show. Bleeding Limeys."

"Should we not be hoofing it out of here, then?" Lavery put forth.

Wiggins the wise was aghast: "In broad daylight? During a major offensive? It'd be the same as committing bloody suicide. We'd not last an hour in open country, lads. But rest easy: I've a plan to get us some transportation." Ending this tale with a wink to his hall-thanes.

Who sat farting *arak*, those trusty retainers, beseeching their leader to round out his rune.

(Which—by way of last night's briefing officer, it emerged—consisted of a French police station not two miles down the road, manned by a handful of Senegalese and one French officer.)

"We'll catch them with their pants down, boys," Wiggins prophesied. "Commandeer a vehicle or two and take the lot back as prisoners."

So bold a design had he drawn for his stalwarts, they mustered their meadpots and drank to the deed.

"Bugger our way back to the border in style, what?" quoth

Wiggins the wonderful. "The effing Limeys will drop a medal on us. Bloody 'eroes, that's what we'll be."

Yet one of their number hight Lavery the leaner, a tall wight and knobby, took issue *en vite*: "And just supposing they decides to fight?"

"Come *on*," cried Wiggins the warlike, his countenance fierce as a falcon in flight. "A bunch of superstitious Abos? They'll turn tail like roos at the first shot."

Then walked over to me with some fatherly advice: "Look, Moses, you and your pal are free to wait 'ere. One of you 'as to guard the wog, anyway. We'll pick you both up on the way out."

"He says?" from Joseph.

"That you should stay and guard the old man," I said. And: "I'll need your revolver."

"Take the damned thing," he told me, washing his hands of me, Wiggins, and the war in general.

Thus we separated. I have no way of knowing if the revolver would have saved him. All I know is that I would have followed Wiggins to hell in order to redeem my pride.

And so we sallied forth.

On the basis of a months-old and at best second-hand intelligence report, most likely purchased from an Arab double agent.

Omitting to cut the telephone wires.

Neglecting to reconnoiter Iskanderun.

The lads walking unsteadily: joking among themselves, strung out like stragglers on both sides of the road.

As fine an assemblage of fuck-ups as ever took the field.

The sun still hung below the mountains although day was unfurling over the sea. Great streaks of pink and lavender in the sky. Gulls dipped and rose above the surf, complaining in their hag-high voices. Far offshore, a ship crawled across the horizon. Underneath the morning coolness you could smell, taste the dry and coppery leaven of impending heat.

Keeping to the road, we skirted the edge of the plateau, and then came a mile-long eastward-looping curve that suddenly bent north to run straight between dense rows of orange trees. Up ahead, an east-west range of foothills towered above the orchard, their gray flanks going brown when the sun broke, splashing light everywhere. The orange trees seemed to shake as their leaves changed from black to green.

Fifteen minutes later we reached the clearing.

Which opened on our left, bordered on the road by a low rock wall some one hundred feet long. Behind the wall: a manicured lawn, dark green and glistening with dew, rising gracefully in two tiers and looking rather like a wide golf tee, at the rear of which, its back to the sea, stood the fort.

Which of course was not a fort at all, but in reality a white-stucco two-story villa with a stone balustrade encircling the veranda on which stood four metal tables protected by canvas umbrellas. A circular flower garden in the center of each grassy tier. A tall hedge separating the lawn from the orange trees. Waist-high rose bushes lining the walk leading from veranda to front gate. The place was like a clubhouse, so tranquil it would not have bowled me over had a man in knickers stepped onto the topmost tier with a brassie in his hand.

Also, in a graveled recess beyond the far end of the wall: one armored car. Seating capapcity: six.

A fact not unperceived by the disgruntled Australians.

But Wiggins was grinning like a madman. "What'd I tell you, lads?" he whispered. Stirred the air with his finger, adding: "Transportytion!" Then scampered off seaward down the grove, taking half the men to attack from the rear while the rest of us climbed through the hedge to make a frontal assault. It certainly appeared that we had, as Wiggins predicted, caught them with their pants down.

Just then the front door opened and a French captain walked abruptly onto the veranda.

Head lowered, buttoning his tunic, he skipped down the steps: a small dapper man of forty or thereabouts with a neat little mustache. Strode briskly along the walk, whistling a *chanson* and fussing with his cap. For a moment I thought he was going to walk right past us, but at the last, as he was placing the cap on his head, his eyes clicked sideways. Whereupon he stopped dead in his tracks: one hand on the visor and the other pressing the crown—looking uncommonly Chaplinesque.

And even more so as his expression shifted rapid-fire from annoyance to brow-lowering disbelief to bug-eyed astonishment. He lowered his hands slowly, flung us a look of reproach, and took off for the villa shouting: *"Gardez-vous!"*

Until Lavery cut him down with two short bursts from the Tommy gun that knocked him over a rose bush. He crumpled face down, one sleeve caught on the thorns, the fingers of his upraised hand clenching and unclenching.

We heard shots from behind the building. Men were screaming.

And then, as the Americans are so fond of saying, the shit really hit the fan.

*

*The General broke for lunch at 11:15—consuming onion soup, escalope du veau, broccoli au gratin, and a peach flan. Afterwards he reclined the seat and took a nap, waking at 2:30 to find the pilot standing over him with worried eyes.*

*"I am afraid we have a problem, sir."*

*"Yes?" he said angrily: embarrassed, his brain clotted with sleep.*

*"Kennedy Airport has just informed me that we can anticipate a holding time of forty-five minutes to an hour."*

*He blinked several times and sat up, bringing the backrest to vertical again. "Well, what of it? Surely you expected some delay at Kennedy on a Friday afternoon."*

*The pilot stared at him with a funereal expression. "Yes, but I did not count on those headwinds I mentioned earlier lasting ninety minutes. We increased our air speed to maintain course, burning up so much extra fuel that our reserve will be almost depleted by the time we are over New York."*

*Wide awake now, the General said: "Well, short of ditching it in the drink, what do you suggest?"*

*"I could identify you," the pilot said doubtfully, "and request a landing priority."*

*"Out of the question. The last thing I want is to draw attention to myself."*

*The pilot nodded, masking his relief. "The only other alternative is to request a change of destination from Kennedy and ask Newark International for clearance to land."*

*"Newark? Why not LaGuardia?"*

*"Their control tower is forecasting the same holding time as Kennedy."*

*The General debated for a moment, then shrugged. "All right, Newark. But I want the Israeli Ambassador notified of the flight-plan change at once."*

*Squaring his shoulders like a matador dedicating a bull, the pilot said: "I will radio Newark every two minutes until they confirm their phone call to the embassy,* mon Général.*"*

*Sitting down at the controls, the pilot whistled under his breath and knocked twice on the mahogany instrument panel. "Radio Kennedy," he told the copilot, "and ask for an emergency change of destination. Then contact Newark International and advise them that we need landing clearance because our fuel supply is running out."*

*The copilot, a much younger man, was confused. He looked at the gauges. "But we have plenty of fuel."*

*"I know," the pilot said. "But the General wants to go to Newark. Would you care to go back and demand an explanation from him?"*

*The copilot made the calls.*

\*

Just had a dream about Ben Gurion, Mollie. Odd to encounter the old reprobate at 30,000 feet. And yet it seems fitting that he should oppose gravity; God knows he spent his lifetime defying practically every law ever written. Here is an item for the miscellaneous files:

1968, an early morning. Ben Gurion was in bed with a cold. Propped upright with pillows. His fierce white hair flaring in all directions. Looking like a cross old owl with his feathers ruffled. As, indeed, they were.

By Lavon. Who stood at the window watching spring climb the humpbacked hills of Jerusalem. A slender, dark, intense, stoop-shouldered man. Saying: "We hated to admit they were there. From the beginning, we spoke of them as children: irresponsible, incapable of running a country. Corrupt, we said; uncivilized; in need of a firm hand."

A storm was gathering on Ben Gurion's brow. "And we were right," he said in a hoarse voice.

Myself in a corner across from the bed. Present at Ben Gurion's almost frantic summons. ("The man un*nerves* me," he had confessed. "I can't contend with him. Lose my temper, start chattering like a monkey.") Wanted me to serve as foil to Lavon's prickly intellect. ("You are the minister of defense, dammit—*defend* me!")

Lavon saying: "No one spoke of dislodging them. Not in public—never in Palestine, at any rate. In New York and Vienna we admitted our intentions; but here, within earshot of the Arabs, we practiced our own version of *katman*: preaching coexistence out loud but declaring in private that they would have to go."

And Ben Gurion reacting with: "Of *course* we did. Justifiably: they would have slaughtered us if we had told the truth." Rolling his eyes in vexation as he realized his *bêtise*.

"And justifiably," Lavon mimicked him. Then going on: "I do not deny the practical considerations, distasteful as they are from a moral viewpoint."

Ben Gurion seemed to erupt beneath the quilts: "Mor*a*lity? The practical consideration was survival. Our position in those days, you'll recall, was tenuous at best. We had to invent our strength—transmogrify the Balfour Declaration into a fleet of British warships and then wave the paper armada at the Arabs to discourage them from killing us in our sleep. We bluffed them. Finessed the British with their own cards. And you expect me to regret it? I'm talking about the formation of *Israel*, not right and wrong. We needed *time*, remember? To consolidate our settlements. Start new ones. Train an army, purchase weapons. Develop an economy. Establish medical facilities, schools. Finance immigration. All of which meant money: and so we begged and borrowed and connived and wheedled and cheated, and built this nation from the ground *up*—out of bricks and mortar and blood, not metaphysics.''

And Lavon saying: ''I am not belittling the achievement—after all, I had a hand in it. What sickens me is the deceit we entered into.''

''You had a hand in that as well, if memory serves,'' Ben Gurion said.

And Lavon saying: ''Yes, I lied through my teeth like a good Zionist.''

''And the Arabs matched us lie for lie,'' Ben Gurion countered. ''From the very start. We needed land. Those sons of probity made us pay through the nose for swampground so malarial the Bedouin avoided it. Places too barren to support a lizard. We bought more sand than you could shovel out of *Florida*. And killed ourselves making it produce. A barrel of Jewish sweat for every inch of reclaimed soil.''

And Lavon saying: ''In the beginning, yes. But these disgraceful confiscations are quite another story.''

Thin ice. Ben Gurion crossed it carefully, skating from one *pro bonum publico* to another: mumbling about abandoned property reverting to the state, the needs of an expanding population, security desiderata—then hung fire and went into a stagy coughing fit.

And Lavon saying: "All illegal measures, nonetheless."

Ben Gurion turned purple: "The land belongs to those who cultivate it, dammit!"

"I wouldn't quote Karl Marx," Lavon said. "Not that line, anyway. It typifies selective morality and the worst kind of sophistry. I am talking about Arabs who pick fruit in orchards they once owned."

The ice was cracking; Ben Gurion, too—staring at Lavon's back like a patriarch of old about to order a prostitute stoned. Slowly, sternly, he said: "We turned this desert into an *oasis*."

And Lavon turned round. Exhibiting that long, serious, gentle face. Saying: "I can do without the parable of the oasis, if you don't mind. A New York audience may snap it up like wolves at raw meat; but unlike them, unlike you also, I was born here—remember? What do Brooklyn Jews think Arabs in Palestine subsisted on for two thousand years—rocks? That there were no olives or dates or figs prior to our coming? That the oranges and wheat and barley and all those vegetables sprouted overnight like the mythical beanstalk? We brought technology to Palestine, not agriculture. We increased the extent of arable land, and at unbelievable sacrifice; but it is the silliest of fabrications to pretend that none existed beforehand—the confiscations are themselves *prima facie* evidence against such pretense. The truth is that the first Jewish settlers would not have lasted six months without Arab aid and advice, on everything from farming to diet and how to dress against the heat. And so, if on your next trip to America you want to use a simile with a bit more bite, you might liken our experience here to that of the Pilgrims and the Massachusetts Indians—who also, incidentally, were driven into obscurity."

And Ben Gurion sputtering: "We brought civilization, modern *in*dusttry, everything from tractors to *toilets* to . . . to a society that was living in the Middle Ages!"

And Lavon replying: "True—but the Arabs should not have had to pay for such improvements by ceding their country to us. Had they been exposed to European ideas and an enlightened program

of education, they might well have accomplished their own indus-
trial revolution.''

And Ben Gurion at his most pontifical: "*Their* country?" Then
hoisting the sacred slogan: "This is Israel—our ancient homeland.''

And Lavon coming back with: "We cannot claim sole right of
ownership to a piece of territory simply because some of our
ancestors once inhabited it. Using the same rationale, the Arabs
could just as easily lay claim to Spain.''

This appealed to Ben Gurion: "Good idea. Let Franco have the
bastards. I'll furnish their transportation.''

And later: "I will not negotiate with a pack of cutthroats," from
Ben Gurion.

And Lavon saying: "The terrorists are not the issue. They have
never been the issue. We run them up the flagpole to avert attention
from the real problem: those refugees cooped up in camps outside
our door. Living in squalor, forgotten, useless, the old waiting to
die, the rest rotting away—their lives reduced to a meaningless
ritual. Not a pretty picture, those haunting, familiar faces behind
the wire. Better to focus on a small number of madmen than a
million innocent victims. Better to bind our conscience tight and
forget that Israel was created as an answer to persecution.''

"It is time we faced up to some hard, unpleasant truths—not the
least of which is that the Palestinians once ruled this country,''
Lavon was saying. "This prerogative was violated in 1948 without
any provocation on their part, in a move that was, in their eyes at
least, an act of total usurpation. And there is no evading this
simple, incontestable fact.''

And Ben Gurion saying: "You want me to give Israel back to
them? Send two million Jews off on another Diaspora?''

And Lavon said: "No—I am asking you to restore their dignity.
We cannot turn back the clock. Neither in all logic can we ask them
to abandon the desire for their homeland. But we can take that first

step toward redressing the wrong we have done in depriving them of rights at least as legitimate as our own. Not only can—must. Our intransigence is an open invitation to the terrorists. Their viciousness in turn makes us more obstinate. We have to put an end to this stupidity—stop gabbling about pedigree and start recognizing that they deserve to live as human beings, too. As long as we remain insensitive to their real predicament, they will go on fighting."

And Ben Gurion saying: "Let them. We can always win wars."

And Lavon falling silent, going to the window, saying: "You may be right. Perhaps we are trapped in a tunnel that has no exit. I leave it for others to find cause for rejoicing in this . . . in the prospect of war arriving with Biblical regularity . . . our children growing up in a country where men can never plant a tree or plow a furrow without a rifle on their backs, an armed camp migrating closer to fascism with each passing year . . . self-righteousness and the law of *lex talionis* become the new religion . . . and how long before we bring the nightmare full circle? . . . we who know more fully than anyone on earth how hatred can be institutionalized and murder made legal, as long as there exists a scapegoat and a legend and a need . . . —how long before *we* issue the armbands?"

And Ben Gurion said: "Words."

*

And Lavery shouted: *"Buggering Jesus, there's a bloody nigger republic in there!"*

Because there were black soldiers in various states of undress bursting onto the veranda with their turbans loose and coiling down their backs like cotton bandage: one man wearing only drawers, others rushing round the north side of the building firing on the run while we scrambled for the wall—losing five men before we reached it, and they would have finished us there and then if it hadn't been for Lavery's Tommy gun, because we must have killed twenty of them before the dark wave broke momentum and washed back inside the villa, only to pin us down promptly from the roof; and so we did "lay siege to the fort" in a manner of speaking, having no place else to go at the moment.

And then Wiggins retreating on the south side through the grove followed by two Aussies, one of whom ran clutching his shoulder; and a second later the man exploded into view: an immense jet-black Senegalese, naked to the waist, his enormous chest muscles rippling as he ran with his head thrown back, uttering a loud trilling high-pitched cry more bird-like than human and holding a machete aloft like a torch as he swooped down on the wounded hindmost Aussie—the blade glinting as it whirled and sank and the Senegalese sidestepping to jerk free and then spinning to continue after the other two while the dying Aussie, blood gouting his tunic, pitched forward and Lavery said: "Dear God."

And Wiggins tearing diagonally out of the trees and crashing through the hedge yelling bloody murder while the other Aussie knelt to make a fight of it, but before he'd jacked a round into the chamber the Senegalese was on top of him: kicking soccer-style to knock the barrel away and then planting himself like a batter and swinging, and then the Aussie kneeling headless and beginning to flop like a chicken as the giant leaped the hedge after Wiggins— who was halfway to the wall and moving remarkably fast on his stubby bowlegs, and the Senegalese eating up the distance between them with long powerful strides, and neither we nor the soldiers in the villa able to fire for fear of hitting our man, and Wiggins' face manic with fear as the Senegalese closed the gap—his keen trilling cry rising suddenly in triumph as Wiggins stumbled and lost his footing and then dove, howling with terror as the Senegalese sprang for him; and then Lavery shouted: "Right!" and rose, emptying the better part of a pan into the man's great torso: he backing up with flailing arms as the bullets whacked into him until he toppled like a tree while Wiggins went squirming over the wall, and by then they'd set up a Hotchkiss gun behind the veranda railing and opened up on us: the wall shaking and shells whanging and rock splinters flying everywhere, and Lavery said: *"We'll catch them with their pants down, lads. . . . They'll turn tail at the first shot."*

And then later two of the Aussies made a dash for the armored car, went down, and the Hotchkiss proceeded to splatter them over the road—which left only the three of us, and Lavery said: "Got any more hot flashes, top?"

And Wiggins conceded: "Right. We're up the ramp."

"Is that a fact, now?" Lavery said.

"Only one thing left to do," said Wiggins the warlord.

"Aye," said Lavery. "Put in for a transfer."

"We'll 'ave to toss in the towel," Wiggins decreed. Gave me an understanding look: "Sorry, Moses. I know it'll be rum for you. But I've my own men to consider."

"Bit late in the day, top," Lavery said. "We can't back out of this one. Killed too many of their mates. Those bloody Moors won't be in any mood for prisoners. We'll be lucky they don't cook us and eat us."

And shortly thereafter Wiggins holding up his handkerchief and shouting: "Surrender! We give up, you bloody Abos!" until he caught a bullet in the wrist.

And the rest is a blur: Lavery hit in the shoulder and turning pale (but still a lovely man, as the Irish say—telling me: "I could do with a jar for sure, Moses"), and Wiggins the woeful blubbering hysterically—and the dust and the heat and the wounded crying in that strange urgent language of hard pain, and the stinking butcher shop smell of death all around us . . . and I guess I snapped, because suddenly I was running in a crouch with Lavery's grenade pouch in my hand, the Hotchkiss swinging on me as I lobbed the first one: the two men at the machine gun following it with wide eyes as it sailed overhead and landed just behind them; and then they were tumbling onto the lawn with the Hotchkiss, but by then I'd heaved two more onto the roof and was making for the north end when Lavery joined me—each of us dropping a grenade through a window and ducking as the glass disintegrated; and then somehow we were inside and there were two soldiers rushing down the stairs and we shot them and then ran into the north wing where we found three dead, eight others on the floor holding their ears from the concussion—and then Lavery was laughing and Wiggins the watchful stood up slowly behind the wall and said: "Now *that's* more like footwork, Moses," and it was over.

Except for the sniper.

\*

And speaking of being ambushed, Mollie. Here's a story I've never told anyone. It was last December. A Sunday: my picture on the front page of the morning paper—another scurrilous attack. The lady prime minister phoned while I was having breakfast. An invitation to her home, pressing matters, one o'clock. I wrote my resignation and then put on my uniform, deciding to go out as I had come in.

She met me at the gate. Wearing a babushka and a gray frock that gave her swollen body the appearance of a canvas-draped keg. (As usual, looking like Lyndon Johnson in drag: the same rumpled nose, eyes combining sadness and cruelty, a bitter mouth. Substituting that babushka for a Stetson would have made the likeness absolutely uncanny.) Took my hand, proffering a downy cheek on which I bestowed a peck. Stepped back, regarding me with baggy smiling eyes, said: "You always look so dashing in uniform."

"An optical illusion," I said, pointing to my patch.

Showed me her vegetable plot. She being Ukranian, it was bordered with flowers. Cut some long-stemmed roses, held them to my nose. Linked her arm in mine as we went up the rear steps. Near the top she faltered, leaning on me—seemed to be in pain, holding her breath with half-shut eyes, and I thought "my God, a heart attack," until she broke wind like an old rhinoceros. Swatting the air behind her haunch as I opened the door.

I handed in my resignation over tea. She slipped on wire-rim glasses to read it; pulled a long face, sighed, placed a hand on her forehead, said finally: "I can't tell you how much I regret this."

I let the lie pass, saying: "I need a rest."

She nodded: "Me, too. Next year," she flipped her spoon

gardenwise, "—out to pasture." Removed the glasses, shook them once like a thermometer as she said: "But my successor will inherit a strong Israel."

I could not let this go by, however. So I said: "For so long as American support continues."

Her face dropped another floor: "Another cryptic prediction?"

"Not prophecy," I told her, "—logic."

She sipped, placed an arrow carefully: "I understand you are becoming a second Jeremiah. What a pity you did not tell us in advance that Israel would suffer five thousand casualties in the war."

"I warned you from the start that they were stronger, better equipped, better trained than anyone imagined," I said. "As I recall, you laughed."

She brushed this aside like a cobweb: "A leader cannot wage war with a defeatist attitude."

"Nor can he or she afford to ignore the facts," I said. "A good general is a realist. Sometimes he gambles, but always with sound appreciation for the odds. And the disagreeable truth is that, this time around, their cards were almost as good as ours."

"Your second-in-command has charged you publicly with dereliction of duty," she said. "*That* is a fact I find difficult to ignore."

"The officer in question," I said, "lost twenty-five percent of his entire force through sheer folly. And against my orders, I might add."

"He claims it was your reluctance to prosecute the battle, your caution in committing reserves, which cost so many lives," she said.

"And you believe him?" I said.

She played a finger along the rim of her cup: "Let us say I am more inclined to his view." Then, her eyes lethal: "Which is why I am selecting him to replace you as minister of defense."

I shook my head: "Forgive me, but promoting a military man for incompetence is highly illogical, and a dangerous mistake."

She slapped the desk, her cup shaking like her voice: "No more dangerous than the speeches you have been making! Ranting about demilitarization and statehood for the Palestinians on the heels of the worst disaster in our history!'' Then lowering the volume: ''You must be mad. This government will never succumb to such radicalism while I control it.''

And I said: ''But you will not always be prime minister.''

She lurched forward, spat: ''And you will *never* be,'' then, aware that she had gone too far, caught herself and added hastily: ''. . . not as long as you advocate such unacceptable ideas.''

''I spoke of recognition for the Palestinians as far back as 1967,'' I reminded her.

She said: ''In 1967, you knew how to win wars.''

And I had had enough: ''We face an enemy whose armament and preparation are as sophisticated as our own. I warned my field staff to expect this, to engage with caution until they had an accurate picture of enemy strength and deployment. Regrettably, several of my field commanders chose to disregard my instructions. Lost in visions of another Six-Day waltz, they overextended themselves and were decoyed into running out of gas, or led by the nose into waiting mortars—trapping three complete battalions. I had my hands full warding off a holocaust. Under the circumstances, five thousand casualties was a miraculously low figure. Tragic, but a portent of things to come if we insist on underestimating them. When armies are equally matched, the contest depends on technique, determination, and luck.''

''Also courage,'' she said pointedly.

I said it standing on my feet: ''No one, Madam Prime Minister, has ever impugned my courage. We have both grown old in the service of Israel—the difference being that you have shed your tears, I my blood.''

*

Also one eye, seven teeth, an upper lip, the bridge of my nose, and two fingers . . . the bullet that shattered the binoculars casing driving the left eyepiece an inch into the orbit, from which it protruded, like some misplaced rhinocerine horn, for the next eight hours; and Wiggins the bold trying with both hands to pull it out as I lay on the roof, until Lavery vowed to shoot him unless he stopped. (Trying also to leave me behind—"What's the use, Irish? Look at 'im, for God's sake. 'E's bloody well 'ad it." And Lavery saying angrily: "Then he'll bloody well die in the car, mate; but make no mistake about it, he's coming with us. Now pick him up." To this day I am convinced that Wiggins only relented because in carrying me piggyback across the lawn he was shielded from the sniper.)

And all because, the Senegalese having had time to call for reinforcements, I'd gone up to the roof with a pair of binoculars Lavery found in the radio room while Wiggins repaired outside, ostensibly to lift the keys to that armored car from the dead Captain—but lifting also his watch and rings and wallet, and in all probability would have expropriated the poor man's boots had not the sniper chased him back into the villa. Yours truly having ascertained that the road was clear in both directions, it was obviously time to be going.

But in the aftermath of battle men behave most unpredictably: some become euphoric, catatonic, are prone to weep, throw fits, take a temporary religious turn, beat their best friends to a pulp—and if in the encounter one has distinguished himself, no matter in how small a way, there comes over him a sense of invincibility: the feeling that he has been touched by the Gods, singled out for special favor, a surety (which lasts exactly until the next action) that he is immune from harm.

Which I suppose accounts in large part for what surely must be reckoned as the crowning goose-brained act of my life.

In any case, having checked the road, I (who have written manuals, you understand, on fieldcraft) next trained the binoculars on the hills, intending of course to locate the sniper. Paying no heed to Lavery's cries of warning; the glint from those lenses an all

but unmissable target for any marksman with a telescope . . .
Practically begging the bastard to pot me.

Later, in the armored car (they'd dumped me on the back seat), I
heard Wiggins in an awe-filled voice say: "Jesus. When those
bloody Druzes finish a man, they *finish* 'im."

"It wasn't the Druzes," Lavery said. "Poor boy—he cut the old
wog loose and then gave him back his knife."

We were motionless, the motor idling. A door opened, shut.
The hollow, wooden ring of footsteps told me we were on the
bridge.

Then Lavery said: "What'll we do with him?"

So I raised up, still in shock, the pain sharp but nothing like it
was to become in the following hours on that bumpy road to
Palestine. Saw Lavery: ashen, holding a severed hand. And then
my vision distorted, the images tripling, filmy, wavering, elongat-
ing fantastically as in those trick mirrors you see in horror houses,
so that what remained of Joseph seemed a grotesque apparition: a
bloody form propped against the railing of the bridge . . . minus
hands and feet, one testicle dangling from his mouth like an oyster.

And Wiggins saying: "You take 'is legs."

I passed out as they dropped him off the bridge.

And that, Mollie, my girl, is the story behind the most famous
wound in the world. Which wrecked my face but made of me, as
one of the more embarrassing biographies would have it, "the
living symbol of Israel," quote, unquote.

*

One last scrap of memorabilia before we land:

Gerda Bloch agreed with my symbol-struck biographer. "It's
true," she told me—this in 1969, she hauntingly thin and bedrid-
den, her long and losing bout with cancer almost at an end, the

larynx deterioration so advanced that her voice was little more than a whisper and I had to sit on the bed, our heads nearly touching, in order to catch her next words: "You *have* become the symbol of this cursed land."

I shook my head and said: "Not me," then made a bad joke: "What *I* am is living proof that plastic surgery has come a long way since 1941."

She laughed—a series of dry respirations which more resembled an infant coughing—and then closed her eyes, falling silent, and, it seemed after a minute or so, asleep as well. I was about to leave when she spoke: "Earlier this year I asked Golda Meir if she would accept the living conditions she and her friends have imposed upon the Palestinians. She of course said no. In *alto voce*. Her exact words, delivered in the usual grave manner, as though she were Moses announcing yet another edict from Mount Sinai, were: 'Because the Jewish people, whose only crime is that they refuse to disappear, deserve at long last a place on this earth where they can live and die in peace.' She was incapable of completing that sentence, of making a simple human extension, of tacking on one small dependent, but all-important clause—and so do the Palestinians. Not unwilling, mind you; inca*pable*. And therein lies the tragedy." Her voice faded out again. Then abruptly: "You are the perfect symbol."

I thought her mind was wandering. " 'Willing to die in order to live?' " I asked playfully, quoting the biography. " 'Wounded but not defeated?' "

"Not because of some pretentious paperback," she said. "Not the fact of your bravery, or the suffering and sacrifice carved into your poor face—those are qualities common to all mankind, Jew and Gentile alike."

"What, then?" I asked her. Fishing for compliments at the feet of the dying.

"Simply"—she took my hand, smiling affectionately to show no insult was intended, and then stripped both my vanity and Israel to the bone—"because you are half-blind."

*

*In the bathroom after the Lear touched down, he removed his eye patch and stared at the cavity: a cone of wrinkled flesh that tapered down to a soft, wet center of yellow pus. He took a cotton swab and wiped off the usual residue of flaky dead skin, then dabbed at the center to soak up the flud. Leaning back, he dripped solution into the cavity with an eye dropper. Then he replaced the patch, washed his face, adjusted his tie, and went back up the aisle to gather his things. The Lear was slowing to a stop. Through the window he saw the Ambassador's limousine pull up beside the plane.*

*The copilot heated the remaining precooked four-course meal and sat down to eat facing the rear of the cabin. "Have they gone?" he asked without turning when Straus reentered the plane.*

*"Yes, thank God," Straus replied.*

*"This crab is magnificent," the copilot said, forking another mound of delicate white meat into his mouth.*

*Straus came up behind him. "Of course. The chef spent fifteen years at Maxim's before entering the Baron's service."*

*The copilot's head bobbed back and forth over the plate. He was vaguely aware of a soft whirring sound followed by a click. "Where are we staying tonight?"*

*"I have reservations in Damascus," Straus told him, placing the silencer an inch from the suddenly stilled head. Adding: "You will remain on board," he shot the copilot twice.*

# Jihad

The scarred man inserted the ear plugs, paid his toll, and then eased the Land Rover ahead a few feet before flicking the ignition cutout switch, oblivious to the mounting chorus of horns at his back as he ground the starter, turning it over and over placidly while he adjusted the rear-view mirror to focus on the lane to his left: watching the Israeli ambassador's limousine (and directly behind it the Cadillac bearing Ahmed and Moussa) inch forward until only four cars separated the limousine from the toll booth, at which point he turned off the cut-out switch, the engine catching instantly, and drove quickly into the tunnel.

Whereupon Ali, standing on the roadway above the portals, clicked the stopwatch going and then raised his binoculars: watching the limousine work gradually up to the toll booth, following the smooth downward glide of the driver's window and the subsequent extension of a uniformed chauffeur's arm (noting the General and the Ambassador conversing in the rear seat), and then the window gliding upward as the limousine slid away to pass glintingly beneath him at +59 seconds, pursued 13 seconds later by the Cadillac, upon whose disappearance he laid the binoculars on the ledge and said: "They are in," into the walkie-talkie; then returned his eyes to the stopwatch, taking little notice of the sudden rattle of gunfire or the ensuing explosions from the south tube, his attention centered on the tiny black dial and its minute convulsive orbit, which he snapped to a close at +100 seconds, saying clearly and sharply into the walkie-talkie: "Now!"

Then took up the binoculars and turned in time to see both bomb casings erupt from the river and rise erratically like canisters shot

135

from a mine-thrower before they lost momentum and went down spinning crazily; he having by then trained the glasses near midstream north of the buoys where the *Vita-Vita* floated, drawing Abdul into fine focus: who stood on the rocking forward deck beside the windlass with his feet wide apart wearing a smile of immense satisfaction and who was raising a hand to shield his eyes from the sun when the arm to which it was attached flew off as both he and the bow (and a split-second later the stern) disintegrated— debris sailing skyward while the cruiser's midsection heaved slug- gishly about and wallowed over on its side amid flames and smoke.

# One

~~~

In the opinion of the Gallup Poll, the assault on the Lincoln Tunnel created overnight a nationwide sense of outrage unmatched since the Japanese sneak attack on Pearl Harbor. The story made the front pages of every newspaper in the country. (Many of which actually likened the event to that distant Hawaiian disaster; one Iowa daily carrying the historical association to its logical conclusion by demanding that Palestine be recognized at once so that Congress could declare war on her.) Accordingly, the President himself quickly appointed a Commission to oversee the official investigation of the tragedy. This distinguished bipartisan panel was eventually to subpoena 603 witnesses whose sworn testimony, comprising 10,000 pages, was subsequently published in 9 volumes that came to be known as "The Jihad Report"—which began with this session on October 26th:

*

*Chairman Baker (glancing right and left to his associates seated at the long table)*: Well, I believe we can proceed. (*Removes his glasses to stare at the witness*) Your name is Michael Sultan?

*Sultan*: Yes.

*Baker*: And you were the supervisor in the control room at the time of the disaster?

137

~~~

*Sultan*: I was the duty officer, yes.

*Abzug (the lone distaff member on the panel; wearing what appears to be a purple velvet sombrero)*: Excuse me, Mr. Chairman. Does that mean you were in *charge* of the Lincoln Tunnel, Mr. Sultan?

*Sultan*: More or less.

*Moynihan (tapping his pencil on the table)*: No hedging, Mr. Sultan, if you please. We are here to weed out the ambiguities surrounding this tragic affair. Confine yourself to specifics.

*Sultan*: I wasn't trying to be ambiguous. Each section has its own chief, who generally runs his own show. My job, primarily, is coordination—insuring that the whole operation works smoothly. In the event of an emergency, however . . .

*Moynihan*: . . . The answer, Mr. Sultan. A simple yes or no will do.

*Sultan*: Yes, then. I was responsible for every function in the complex.

*Baker*: Fine. Now, Mr. Sultan, before we go any further I would like to make perfectly clear that, although you are under oath, this is not a judicial proceeding. As my colleague (*nods to Moynihan*) has pointed out, our task is to try and arrive at a precise understanding of what transpired in the Lincoln Tunnel on October eighteenth. Information, then, is our paramount goal. But we are not a tribunal, and this is not a witch hunt. Is that understood?

*Sultan*: Yes.

*Baker*: Good. Now (*replaces his glasses to look briefly at his notes*) . . . according to the FBI's preliminary report, you were an eyewitness to most of what went on inside the tunnel. Is that a fair statement?

*Sultan*: Well, there were three computer technicians on duty at the time, and they—that is, all four of us—were scanning the monitors for the first three or four minutes. I probably saw more than anyone from start to finish, though.

*Baker*: We of course intend to call your assistants in the near future. Today, however, we would simply like to establish a general idea of the sequence of events. I would like you, therefore, to tell us, to the best of your recollection, what happened that afternoon.

*Abzug*: Forgive me, Mr. Chairman. From start to finish, you said, Mr. Sultan. The cameras functioned up to the end?

*Sultan*: Most of them, yes. The lights, too. Both are wired through the walls and were not damaged when the bombs went off.

*Jackson*: Mr. Chairman, if I may? How clear was the image on those television screens, Mr. Sultan?

*Sultan*: Very distinct in the beginning. Toward the end the lenses were sweating and the quality deteriorated somewhat due to distortion. But by then there were only those three survivors, less than fifteen feet from the camera, and we had no difficulty following their movements.

*Baker*: Very well. And now, if there are no further questions . . . you may begin, Mr. Sultan.

*Sultan*: All right. But first, I would like you to appreciate that this was Friday, rush hour, and the center tube was closed. That is to say, the commuter overload was heavier than Labor Day. From where I sat it looked something like the Oklahoma Land Rush in slow motion.

*Moynihan*: Mr. Sultan, everyone here is well acquainted with rush hour at the Lincoln Tunnel, I assure you. (*To the table at large*) However, I did enjoy the simile.

*Sultan*: The point I was trying to make, Mr. Chairman, is that conditions outside had much to do with what happened in the tunnel.

*Baker*: Undoubtedly, Mr. Sultan. But that will become clearer as we progress. Now—when did you first notice that something was wrong?

*Sultan*: When he threw his hat out the window.

*Baker*: I beg your pardon.

*Sultan*: The man driving the Land Rover—he was wearing a wide-brimmed hat. He took it off and tossed it into the roadway a few moments after he entered the tube.

*Abzug*: Why on earth did he do *that*?

*Sultan*: Because underneath he was wearing some kind of turban. Spotted, with a long tail—I could see it flapping as he drove. By then he was going nearly sixty miles an hour.

*Moynihan*: That particular turban, Mr. Sultan, is called a *keffiyeh*. Most Palestinian terrorists wear one.

*Sultan*: I don't know much about Palestinians.

*Moynihan*: No, I suppose not. Tunnels are your specialty. *(Begins jotting down notes, addressing Sultan without looking at him)* You said sixty miles an hour. I take it the tube was fairly congested?

*Sultan*: Packed.

*Moynihan*: The vehicles just crawling along, close together?

*Sultan*: Ten miles an hour, at intervals of around fifty feet.

*Moynihan*: And this fellow simply went flying through them as though he were on a motorcycle.

*Sultan*: He maneuvered the Land Rover expertly, if that is what you mean.

*Moynihan* (*looking up quickly*): I am not interested in his *skill*, Mr. Sultan. The question is: what did you do about it?

*Sultan*: What would you have had me do—ask one of the officers inside to jump onto the roadway and flag him down? Lots of people speed in the tunnel. Junkies, drunkies, maniacs, the suicide fringe. Some ride the accelerator unconsciously in a mild fit of claustrophobia. We have to sit by and watch all sorts of stunts in the course of an average month. Weavers, drag racers, clowns betting on how many cars they can pass, kids making love at the wheel . . .

*Baker*: . . . What exactly *did* you do, Mr. Sultan?

*Sultan*: We have a direct line to the police units at both portals, so I pushed the intercom and told New York we had a crazy man in the tube. Ordinarily, they would have stopped him on his way out and slapped him with a ticket. But of course he never came out. Instead he slowed down approximately two hundred yards from the exit ramp on the Manhattan side and pulled alongside a pickup that was traveling in the left lane. And then he killed the driver with a machine gun.

*Baker*: He fired a machine gun with one arm? Isn't that rather difficult?

*Stennis*: According to the FB*I*, Mr. Chairman, it wasn't a machine gun; it was an M-16, which has a selector switch on the left side near the pistol grip that allows one to choose either automatic or *semi*automatic fire. Which means that it could be operated semiautomatically with one arm, I sup*pose*, although hitting anything in the process from a moving automobile (*faces Sultan*) would be extremely proble*matic*.

*Sultan*: I never said he used one arm.

*Stennis*: Oh.

*Sultan*: He let go of the steering wheel and started shooting, that's all. They were only doing ten miles an hour. I saw glass fragments flying as the passenger window shattered. I also saw the driver of the pickup throw up his hands as he was struck.

*Baker*: What happened then, Mr. Sultan?

*Sultan*: The pickup veered into the north wall and stopped. The killer stopped beside it and stepped out, changing clips. He opened fire on the two approaching cars, which were braking down to see what the trouble was. He killed both drivers, one of whom was a woman. At least I assumed they were dead—the bullets punched a small hole in both windshields, throwing them back against the seat, and neither one moved as the cars came to a stop. He then swung left and wounded the patrolman coming out of his catwalk booth, some one hundred feet west. I saw the officer fall into the roadway. By then the killer had unhooked two grenades from his belt and lobbed one at each car, diving into the Land Rover as they went off. Both vehicles—what was left of them—caught fire. I saw the next pair of oncoming cars run into each other, either from panic or the force of the explosions. They were tangled together about ten feet behind the fires. The killer overhanded a grenade at them from the driver's seat and then started for the ramp. The blast caused his rear end to fishtail, but he kept on going.

*Baker*: How long did all of this take, Mr. Sultan?

*Sultan*: No more than thirty seconds. Less, I would say. It happened very fast.

*Goldwater*: That last grenade he threw—what effect did it have, Mr. Sultan?

*Sultan* (*looks down for a second*): All four cars were burning, I recall. One was standing on end. The next pair of eastbound cars were perhaps ten feet from the fires and trying to back away . . . and that semi attempted to crash between them but ended up dragging both along, sparks flying everywhere, until all three rammed into the burning cars . . . I took this all in at a glance, really; by that time my attention was on the action in the Jersey entrance. (*Looks down again*)

*Baker* (*waiting*): As is ours, Mr. Sultan. (*Smiles patiently at Sultan's uncomprehending expression*) Thirty seconds have elapsed; we are in the Jersey entrance. Please continue.

*Sultan*: The Cadillac with those two terrorists inside had gone into a right-hand skid halfway through the curve, closing off both lanes before I picked it up on the monitors. The man on the passenger side was shooting into the closest cars. Then he leaned far out of the window and tossed three grenades, one right after the other, and the Cadillac wheeled left and spun around the bend. The explosions (I could hear them, by the way) blew out one of the two entrance cameras. The next one up was located above the ramp, almost directly across from those two killers—because the driver (the bearded one, dressed like a chauffeur) stopped the Cadillac sideways near the top of the ramp, bringing it around with the steering side facing the portal. He then got out and came over to help the other one remove two boxes—one containing ammunition clips, the other grenades.

*Javits*: How much time, roughly, did this business in Jersey take, Mr. Sultan?

*Sultan*: Offhand, I would estimate twenty, twenty-five seconds.

*Javits*: And that terrorist at the New York end—what had become of him?

*Sultan*: By then the Land Rover was also sitting broadside at the top of the ramp.

*Javits (enunciating carefully, as if trying to memorize the question)*: Then what you are telling us, Mr. Sultan, is that three men seized the Lincoln Tunnel in less than sixty seconds?

*Sultan*: Certainly no more than that.

*Baker*: What happened next, Mr. Sultan?

*Sultan*: The bombs went off.

\*

. . . Smashing two holes 30 inches in circumference a few yards in from each ramp through which water under 9 tons of pressure literally exploded at the rate of 3500 gallons per second—the 2 high-angle swollen jets bursting as they struck the pavement and roared onward to fan out in a thrashing sibilant mass moving 48.6 miles an hour like two flash floods crashing down a dry arroyo except that the walls of this channel were smooth as glass and the bed dead-level and moreover empty for the first 800 feet on the Jersey side, and consequently within 60 seconds the eastward surge was ankle-deep and considerably stronger than a water cannon used for crowd dispersal; and since we are speaking of the center-mile between both ramps and therefore a capacity of 15,000,000 gallons it followed that since more than 1,000,000 gallons were pumping in every 5 minutes, the level was going to rise 3½ feet each quarter-hour and the tube itself was going to fill in 72 minutes. . . .

# Two

~~

"Our information on that scarred terrorist is rather sketchy," the Interrogator (this still in London on the 26th of October) was saying. He opened a dossier. "We know that he was born in 1942—in Jerusalem, no less."

George (arms free but still bound to the chair from his waist down) took another sip of coffee; said: "A stone's throw from Herod's retaining wall, in fact"; and went back to massaging the strap-marks on his wrists.

"Parents of peasant origin. Father began life as a laborer, became an assistant tailor, then a cloth merchant. An enterprising sort."

"Palestinians," George said complacently, "are known as the Jews of the Arab world."

The Interrogator examined the nails of his left hand for a moment. "The family moved to Ramallah and took up farming in 1947. Father disappeared in 1948, presumably killed in battle during the War of Independence. Shortly thereafter, the family (consisting of him, an older brother and sister, and the mother) migrated to Amman as refugees. They spent the winter in Amman, where in some fashion the brother disappeared. The remaining members turned up at a camp in Jarash in early 1949. The sister died sometime that year, cause unknown. In 1950 he and his mother hired out as farm laborers in El-Shuna, where they lived until 1956, when his mother was killed during an Israeli air attack, and he suffered the burns resulting in his disfigurement." He looked up from the folder. "Have I left out anything so far?"

George finished the coffee before replying. " 'Migration' seems a bit euphemistic, under the circumstances. We are, after all, talking about an Exodus, one sharing, moreover, the same point of departure as the original Diaspora—although in this case, of course, the land was ours by law and not through any circumlocution of Deuteronomy. They were driven out, expelled."

"Very well," the Interrogator compromised, "—how about 'fled'?"

George nodded to himself, looked away, said: "Yes. On foot. Following dun-colored, winding mountain roads, the dust a foot deep. Not walking so much as being swept along by the herd's momentum: one of those timeless rag-tag columns with their belongings in bundles (the past and future knotted together with string and carried on the head), pulling those small wooden-wheeled carts that seem designed for humanity's dispossessed, a few lucky ones with donkeys. They may have had the fortune to spend that first night in a cave—the children spooned into each other beneath their mother's shawl, listening to the wind and those unlucky women giving birth outside in the dark. The second day would have found them on the flat-topped, reddish hills of Jordan, where they probably spent the night in the open (having fallen behind, of course, because of the children, the caves full by the time they caught up with the rest), sleeping in a grove of leafless poplars: white and fragile as birch trees. And after that came those ruinous little Jordanian towns, much knocking on doors to ask bread from stone-faced mountain people; and all this time the dead along the roads: people bloated beyond belief, blackened, eyeless, burst—their limbs and features gnawed off by wild dogs who followed the herd like hyenas (waiting for stragglers, weaklings): and toward the end (the herd thinning in inverse proportion as the pack increased)—toward the end the dogs grew bolder, shameless, tearing at the dying in broad daylight like sharks in a frenzy.

"It took ten days to walk to Amman, which at that time was little more than a huge village with a small main avenue of mud. The entire family, having no relatives or money, became beggars. Street-sleepers. Standing in line outside restaurants to eat what the paying customers left on their plates. Eaters of roaches, worms—the rat population of Amman declining by one-third during this period. Barn-dwellers: listening to horses groaning in sleep while their mother groaned under an overseer—paying for their bed and board in the ancient manner. Such windfalls would not have come their way too often, however, for the mother could simulate enthusiasm but not youth, not beauty (not any more: in her forties, haggard, worn-out from bearing the children as well as a like number of stillborns—dried-up, bent from a lifetime of labor, teeth missing, her breasts hanging down like deflated balloons); and suddenly it was winter, which is most bitter in Amman. Wind froze the mud into furrows; cold rain filled them with ice. They lived in a one-room hovel made of mud and branches. And the brother (he was nine, by the way) had fallen sick: intestinal parasites and exposure combining to make the usual inroads on his lungs. Thus the daughter.

"Who was thirteen, nubile, smooth-skinned, her hips and breasts beginning to swell despite malnutrition. So the mother pandered her, bartered that budding vagina to the rude instrument of any man with enough money to pay for an extra blanket, a little medicine; but more often settling for a few scraps of meat or some potatoes to put in the broth, because the men of Amman prefer young boys, and money, like medicine, was scarce.

"And before long the brother had developed a deep cough that seemed to cut through his entire body, had grown delirious: his face like fire, the hair plastered to his brow, his tongue yellow and covered with sores; and all the mother could do was sponge him and croon and hold him down during the convulsions and weep when he opened his eyes, the body relaxing as he smiled for the last time and filled the blanket with shit. By that time the daughter had gonorrhea and was pregnant.

"Toward the end of winter they walked to Jarash, where there was a temporary UN camp (currently celebrating its twenty-fifth anniversary), which meant that the daughter would receive free medical attention. They were given a tent, flour, and the opportunity to share three water pumps with seven thousand other refugees. The doctor, a German woman who came twice a month, managed to cure the gonorrhea but unfortunately was absent the night the daughter aborted; and hence did not witness the mother holding a candle in the tent and keening in the manner of Palestinian women as her daughter heaved and thrashed (two old men holding her shoulders while the midwife prodded and pulled), finally squeezing forth a dead fetus that slipped out like a red toad, blood spilling after it like water from a tap and the mother covering her ears as the girl screamed herself to death.

"And finally, as you well know, in 1956 the Israeli planes dropped napalm on the citizens of El-Shuna. He lost consciousness, woke in the dark to find himself laid out for burial along with dozens of charred bodies, one of whom was his mother. He was fourteen years old, completely alone, with half his face burned off. And so he ran away—taking refuge in the Salt Mountains, where he lived wild for the next two months until a band of guerrillas operating in the hills found him and took him in."

George turned back to the Interrogator with a pleasant smile. "That's how much you left out."

# Three

~~~

*Baker (taking in the table with a revolving glance)*: Before going any further, I think it would be wise to recapitulate the developments prior to those bomb explosions. If you'll just bear with me a moment, then *(reads from a list, stepping his finger down the page to mark each stage)*: The Land Rover sits above the Manhattan exit ramp; the Cadillac in a similar position on the Jersey side. The Ambassador's limousine, being one of the last cars to enter, is several hundred feet inside the Tunnel, proceeding eastward. The Jersey entrance is jammed with burning cars; and at the other end, about one hundred feet west of the Manhattan exit ramp, a group of vehicles is burning near that semi-trailer. *(Looks up)* Any comment?

*Moynihan*: Mr. Chairman, I for one believe it is high time we shifted our sights from the undeniable efficiency of the terrorists and allowed Mr. Sultan to explain what steps, if any, he was taking to remedy the situation.

*Baker*: Would you respond to that, Mr. Sultan?

*Sultan (staring at Moynihan)*: Gladly. I would like you to bear in mind two facts, though, before I begin. One: police who work in tunnels are traffic specialists, not SWAT teams. In general, they are approaching middle age. Most have never been nearer a shoot-out than the pistol range. For example, of the seventeen

148

~~

officers on duty that afternoon (seven at each portal, three inside), only two had ever participated in a gun battle, and both of these men acquired their experience from the Korean War. In addition, the only weapon they wield is a .38-caliber pistol. Combat readiness, in short, has never been considered part of their job. The only enemy a tunnel cop trains to fight is down-time. Two: they were up against cold-blooded professionals—men not only better armed but on a suicide mission as well. . . .

*Moynihan*: . . . Enough extenuation, Mr. Sultan. The point at issue, in any case, is not *their* amateur status, but yours.

*Sultan*: *Look*, pal . . .

*Baker*: . . . Just a moment, gentlemen. We have no time for personalities in these hearings. Please go on with your account now, Mr. Sultan.

*Sultan* (*eyes lowered, as if talking to himself*): They had it all figured out, you know. They'd planned my moves in advance as well as theirs. For example, to go back to the beginning: once the shooting started, I told the New York end to clear the exit loop immediately, which meant shunting cars right and left as they came out and tying up the approach—which was exactly what the terrorists wanted. (*Looks up*) At the same time, I ordered two officers to move inside and stop that killer in the Land Rover before he came out, because at that point I assumed he would try to escape, and I didn't want a gun battle on the approach. That's where matters stood when the trouble started in Jersey.

There, smoke and motorists abandoning their cars were pouring from the south portal in equal amounts. Several officers had already started carrying out the dead and wounded; others were spraying foam on the fires.

After informing the Jersey unit commander of the situation in New York (by then the Land Rover was parked sideways above the ramp), I told him to clear one entrance lane and get an assault team ready. Just then that killer in New York shot to death those two patrolmen I'd ordered inside. And then the bombs went off. . . .

I don't know how long I stared at the monitors—ten seconds,

something like that. I was paralyzed. More like mesmerized, I guess. Couldn't make myself believe it was real. One of the computer technicians was shouting, pointing at the Jersey entrance, when I snapped out of it. He was saying: "Oh, Jesus, no"; and then I saw three policemen coming around the final bend in front of that Cadillac.

With drawn pistols. Walking close together, of course. Making a nice slow-moving target. Both killers were crouched down, one behind each wheel—invisible, waiting. The Jersey commander hadn't sent them: they'd gone in on their own to investigate after putting out the fires. Neglecting the normal procedure of taking along a walkie-talkie, so there was no time to warn them. The killers let them come to within twenty feet and then shot them down.

While they were dying, I told both units to get the Pettibones ready.

*Moynihan*: And what, pray tell, is a Pettibone, Mr. Sultan?

*Sultan*: A snowplow. My idea was to ram the killers. The operator's cage has a metal front panel which offered some protection, and I thought by raising the blade to form a shield and sending an extra officer along to ride shotgun, that we at least had a chance. They were still towing out cars in Jersey, so we tried the New York end first.

*Stennis*: Under the circumstances, Mr. Sultan, that was, in my opinion, a brilliant idea.

*Sultan*: It was a fiasco. They made it around the curve, the guard peppering that Land Rover with bullets. But that's as far as they got. The killer didn't even fire back. He simply relied on a pair of grenades, which demolished the cage and blew off the right front wheel—reducing the New York unit to three men and creating a roadblock in the exit loop.

*Javits*: How much time are we talking about now, Mr. Sultan?

*Sultan*: Three minutes. The bombs went off at 5:17, and the Pettibone blew up at 5:20 by my clock.

*Moynihan*: One moment, Mr. Sultan. If you were in such a state of shock when the bombs exploded, how did you muster the presence of mind to note the time?

*Sultan*: I checked the clock at 5:20; the 5:17 figure was reported to police by a shad boat skipper who was running down the New York side when one of the bomb casings shot out of the river just off his bow. He also dropped a buoy overboard, which marked the spot for the sand barges.

*Baker*: And we are getting ahead of our story. Apropos of that shad boat, Mr. Sultan, let's return to 5:17. What happened to those people trapped in the tunnel?

*Sultan*: I'd better explain what took place before the bombs went off. Starting with that semi (*shakes his head bitterly*)—which practically sealed the entire eastern end of the tube.

*

. . . Because the trailer broke off and jacknifed to swing sideways in the right lane: mowing down 50 feet of railing until it caught up with (and crashed into) the cab and stopped with its rear end mashed over the catwalk and wedged tight against the south wall; the cab meanwhile having gone airborne upon impact: lunging up in the left lane and smashing against the ceiling, tearing out a metal grate in one of the overhead exhaust vents and crushing the driver to death before it crunched down on a car underneath and came to rest still pointing toward New York but with its front wheels now off the pavement and the hood canted up less than 5 feet from the ceiling. . . .

*

*Baker*: If I understand correctly, then, Mr. Sultan, this trailer blocked the catwalk.

*Sultan* (*nods*): And the right lane as well. And the cab blocked the left lane. Anyone trying to escape eastward had to climb over, or crawl under, that semi rig. And pick their way through a scrap heap on the other side: those four cars the killer demolished plus the two the semi dragged with it—all piled together with that pickup sitting on top.

*Abzug*: I find it strange, Mr. Sultan, that not one car was able to turn around and drive back out the Jersey portal. How do you account for that?

*Sultan*: The noise, for one thing. Sound waves reverberate in a tunnel. It's like being inside a bell. Those explosions at the Jersey end (which, as I mentioned, were audible in the control room) echoed throughout the tube. That may give you an idea of the volume level near the entrance—and the last car in, don't forget, had only gone about two hundred feet when the fireworks started. In any event, the motorists at the tail end hit the gas, setting off a chain reaction that produced a virtual stampede of frightened people toward New York—where of course fifty rows of cars had by now come to a standstill: a number of them at the head of the line already trying to turn back. Both ends, so to speak, met in the middle. (*Holds up both hands, brings them slowly together*.) Like an accordion. Two hundred and sixteen cars: half of them stopped, a third coming on behind at high speed. The result was sheer pandemonium. It looked like some kind of demolition derby: cars rolling, being sideswiped, spinning like tops, doing flips, coming apart; bodies catapulting through the windshields or flying out of open doors; metal grinding metal, pounding itself into jagged piles of scrap in at least a hundred separate collisions. Three cars jumped the catwalk rail. The roadway was blocked in a dozen places even before the bombs exploded. And the water finished the job by triggering a mad brief scramble at the Jersey end: twenty-five cars, most of them bouncing around in reverse, trying to squeeze through two lanes from ten different angles, and all of them becoming hopelessly entangled in a kind of Keystone Kops finale. After that, the only way out was on foot.

*Stennis*: By way of the catwalk, I presume, as opposed to the roadway, Mr. Sultan?

*Sultan*: They had to reach the catwalk first. By the time most of them left their cars the water was six to eight inches deep, and incredibly swift. A lot of people, many of them regrettably children, were swept off their feet. Once down, it was almost impossible to get back up, even for adults. The current washed them

around like driftwood. Many must have been battered unconscious, I suppose, or suffered broken bones. At any rate, the
majority never stood up again.

*Javits*: Could you put a figure to that majority, Mr. Sultan?

*Sultan*: One hundred, perhaps. There were bodies everywhere.

*Abzug* (*under her breath*): Good God.

*Baker*: According to the FBI, Mr. Sultan, fifty-one bodies were
recovered from the New York ramp.

*Sultan*: That sounds about right.

*Baker*: How did they die?

*Sultan*: The killer was waiting for them.

*Jackson*: He shot down fifty-one defenseless people?

*Sultan*: Yes. And threw grenades at them.

*Moynihan*: I hate to belabor the point, Mr. Sultan, but could you
tell us what *you* were doing in the interim?

*Sultan*: I sent two more officers inside, hoping they could pin
him down—get his attention away from the people trying to
escape. But the odds were all in his favor. Our closest vantage
point was of course the Pettibone, which still left seventy feet of
open roadway to that Land Rover—and it was armor-plated, in
case you didn't know. They might as well have thrown darts at the
damned thing. All the killer had to do was stay put and keep an
occasional eye on them. And wait. He knew sooner or later they
would try to rush him; knew they couldn't stand to watch the
slaughter for long. So when it happened, he was ready. He dropped
them both about fifteen feet from the Pettibone.

*Javits*: Let me see if I have this straight, Mr. Sultan. That
semi-trailer formed a barrier across the catwalk which forced most
of the people to head for Jersey?

*Sultan*: What happened on the catwalk was similar to what
occurred in the roadway. That is, the Jersey crowd started for New
York, and vice versa. At the New York end people swarmed
behind that trailer for several minutes: punching and elbowing,
jockeying for a hand-hold—but since it was in effect a seven-foot
wall of ragged steel, only a few were able to scale it. The rest
reversed direction for Jersey. Again, in a manner of speaking, both

ends met in the middle. You must understand that they had been reduced to an ugly terrified mob with only one thought in its head: how to get out. What happened next is hard to describe. It was like hand-to-hand combat. Scores of people were knocked or thrown into the roadway. Into eighteen inches of water that was already swirling over the catwalk where the two currents came crashing together.

*Jackson*: Thrown? Intentionally?

*Sultan*: Yes.

*Javits*: But somehow the momentum swung toward Jersey?

*Sultan*: After a minute or so, yes.

*Javits* (*checking his figures*): We are talking about . . . approximately two hundred and ninety people still left alive.

*Sultan*: The number thinned down by one-third before they started for the Jersey end.

*Javits*: How long did it take them to get there?

*Sultan*: They didn't come all at once. With three cars straddling it at intervals, the catwalk had become an obstacle course. The first group showed up around 5:27.

*Javits*: What happened when they got to the ramp?

*Sultan*: They never made it that far. There were two killers on the Jersey side, remember. One to keep people out, another to keep them in. At 5:22 the bearded one went down into the tunnel carrying an armload of ammunition clips. He planted himself near the end of the catwalk. Then, like his counterpart over in New York, he simply waited for them to come.

*Moynihan*: I trust you found a better way to occupy *your* time, Mr. Sultan.

*Sultan*: The other Pettibone was heading down a clear left lane two minutes later with all four remaining officers from the Jersey units aboard. They swung around the curve so quickly that the killer behind that Cadillac did not have time to react until they were forty feet away. Yet even so, he finished the driver and another officer before the blade overturned the Cadillac and sent it skidding down the ramp dragging the killer along. For a second I thought we had them. The second killer, he must have been wearing earplugs, or perhaps that water spout drowned out the noise—in any case, he didn't realize anything was wrong until the Cadillac and his pal came sailing past below him. Unfortunately, one of the surviving policemen had been thrown from the Pettibone. He was lying on the ramp; appeared to have a broken leg; I couldn't see him clearly. And the other officer made the fatal mistake of jumping down to help him. The bearded man emptied one clip and part of another into them. And that was that.

*Javits*: Why did you involve the entire unit in one strike, Mr. Sultan?

*Sultan*: After what happened on the New York ramp, I really had no other choice. Besides, just before the Pettibone went in I sent for two officers from the Dairy Queen to serve as reinforcements. But they didn't make it to the portal until 5:29, and by then, it was all but over.

*Abzug*: Are you saying this bearded fellow killed over two hundred people?

*Sultan*: More like sixty. The rest turned back.

*Jackson*: Toward New York? A mile away?

*Sultan*: It was either that, or take their chances with a wall of bullets.

*Jackson*: How many made it to New York?

*Sultan*: None. They had covered less than six hundred yards before the water caught them. At 5:34 it boiled over the catwalk like a riptide and started pulling them off by the dozens. In sixty seconds there was no one left. Except for a patrolman who had been on duty in that booth on the Jersey side. He climbed up on the roof.

*Jackson*: Why didn't some of the others join him, for God's sake?

*Sultan*: He wouldn't let them. He clubbed their hands with his pistol. Shot several in the face who refused to let go. Don't ask me why. I can only assume that, like many, he had gone mad.

*Baker* (*breaking the silence*): The end came quickly, Mr. Sultan?

*Sultan*: For most. Some anchored themselves to cars. A few

clung to the railing for a time. But the water was freezing. Forty-eight degrees. Hypothermia set in rapidly. The cold literally paralyzed them. They slipped away one by one over a period of ten minutes.

*Moynihan*: Did it at no time occur to you, Mr. Sultan, to ask for outside assistance?

*Sultan*: Senator Moynihan, three minutes after those bombs went off I had two of my assistants phoning Maydays to every law enforcement agency within a radius of forty miles. However, as I tried to explain an hour ago, conditions outside the tunnel erased the possibility of any immediate help.

*Baker*: Why don't we go into that now, Mr. Sultan?

*Sultan*: The center tube, as you know, was boarded off. Inside, fifty workmen were finishing concrete near the New York end. Ninety yards of concrete. They poured the last yard at five o'clock. So they were troweling and blading; cleaning the mixers, the hoses, a few men up front setting forms for the next shift—when they heard the explosions. And of course they dropped everything and vacated the premises, leaving ninety yards of wet concrete stretching for two hundred and seventy feet in their wake. By now word was spreading through the north tube.

Which was full, the cars sardined bumper-to-bumper in two mile-long rows of edgy people. Because it gets to you, thinking about the river over your head, especially coming down from that last martini. The tube is hot, muggy; people sweat, get itchy, pound their horns. Kids begin to cry. And there are always those with white knuckles staring at the walls.

It started with a few drivers at each end who got out of their cars after the explosions and ran to the portals to see what was going on. Saw the smoke, heard the screaming. Then came flying back inside to get their families or warn their car pool. And pass the word. Specifics don't matter in a situation like that; all it takes is the barest suggestion, the slightest hint, to create panic. Fear ignited them like a spark in a gas-filled room. After that, like those people in the south tube, all they could think of was getting out.

The result was a mass of humanity charging out of both portals, which left the north tube crammed with abandoned cars. The center tube was equally impassable. We would have needed a tank to cross two hundred and seventy feet of soft concrete.

This phase took about five minutes.

By which time the Jersey approach lanes were backed up for two miles on Interstate 495. Over in New York the cars were strung out in a column that was growing longer every minute: running up the ramp and on past Ninth Avenue, branching out along Thirty-fourth and Thirty-fifth Streets—mushrooming, radiating outward through the midtown area. Within fifteen minutes there were six thousand cars stymied in the lower streets alone. And to make things worse, it was getting dark. In other words, it took them less than a quarter of an hour to fix things so that no one was going to reach the tunnel except by helicopter or on foot.

*Baker*: I believe we see your point, Mr. Sultan. Now—I would like to clear up one small item before we get back to the tunnel. When did you request those sand barges?

*Sultan*: 5:20—right after that Pettibone blew up. I asked the harbor police to round up a pair of divers and four barges.

*Baker*: The idea being to unload sand over the holes and cut off the water?

*Sultan*: Yes. They promised to have them there by 6:15.

*Baker*: And yet you saw no reason to inform the harbor authorities when the water stopped by itself on the New York side?

*Sultan*: Not at first. It didn't stop completely, to begin with. It slowed down to a trickle, but that was no guarantee the silt wouldn't slide again and bring the river back at any moment. Later on, when I tried to postpone the drop, harbor control had lost radio contact with the patrol boat escorting those barges.

*Baker*: I see. (*Consulting his notes*) The FBI states that you managed to drive that terrorist from the New York ramp somewhere around 5:35. (*Looks up*) But they make no mention of how you went about it.

*Sultan*: I had little to do with it. Two detectives from one of the

Manhattan precincts got rid of him.

*Moynihan*: And how did they arrive so quickly, Mr. Sultan—by parachute?

*Sultan*: Their squad car was stranded in the north tube. They volunteered their services to the New York unit at 5:30. They, too, were armed with M-16's, by the way. After trading a few shots with that killer, one of them improvised a Molotov cocktail out of a big coke bottle filled with gas and wrapped in a saturated tee-shirt. Then, while his partner laid down covering fire, he ran out from behind the Pettibone, sprinted a few yards down the roadway, and let fly.

The next thing I knew, the Land Rover was covered with flames and that killer was a human torch. He ran back into the tunnel beating at his clothes. I saw him stumble into the water. Then that box of grenades suddenly exploded, lifting that Land Rover into the air and blowing out both entryway cameras, and I lost track of him. The nearest camera still working was the one across from that semi cab, a hundred feet from the ramp—and from that distance it was impossible to pick him out among the bodies. I simply figured he'd gone under and was done for. But he had nine lives, as it turned out.

# Four

~~

The Interrogator closed the dossier with an air of finality. "Would that we could continue with this morbid eulogy; but, unhappily, our time together is almost at an end."

"I'll try to master my grief," George told him.

Taking up the coffee pot, the Interrogator said: "One last shot of paint remover?"

George shook his head. "How about a couple of questions instead?"

The Interrogator swung the pot outward, nodded magnanimously.

"First," said George, "—the General: how did you persuade him to negotiate the treaty? We were under the impression he had washed his hands of politics after the October War."

"Old politicians never die, they simply lose their constituency," the Interrogator said. Then: "We offered him the prime ministership."

George smiled perceptively. "The one post which has always eluded him. Tempting bait, I must admit."

"You forget that he was also a military man, and an Israeli born and bred."

"In Degania, no less," George said respectfully. "Mother of Kibbutzim. Hallowed ground, the hero's birthplace. Making him a sabra's sabra, the seventh son of a seventh son—nobility deriving from a clause in the deed, acquired with the property like some hidden vein of gold. Comparable in a way to having been whelped on the beach while the Pilgrims unloaded the Mayflower.''

The Interrogator's face was rigid. ''I was of course referring to his sense of patriotic duty.''

''Of course. Yaweh and the sacred soil. Once more into the breach, and all that. Except that this time, if you will forgive the pun, he did not know the breech was loaded. Which brings me to the second question.''

The Interrogator tapped his wristwatch. ''Be brief.''

''The death of Straus,'' George said, ''I'll accept as given. He was conspicuous, alone in Damascus, an easy mark. We anticipated that one of your assassination teams would hit him quickly—although pulling it off two days after the incident in New York was, under the circumstances, rather blinding speed even for a people who pride themselves on swift retribution. Still, I saw nothing inordinate in his execution. Ali, however, was an entirely different story. I personally recruited him from that bank in Beirut. He had no previous connection with the Organization, no file, nothing. Moreover, during the month and a half prior to his departure for New York, he lived in seclusion in my Paris flat.''

The Interrogator's eyebrows went up a fraction. ''Am I to assume that you, too, partook of the forbidden fruit?''

''Till I was blue in the face,'' George assured him. ''But the point is: no one, not even the Committee, could have led your men to Ali. No one, that is, except myself. And I never saw him again after the eighteenth. Yet somehow you found and killed him in Beirut on the very same day that Straus met his maker in Damascus. Ali's death, therefore, came as quite a shock. The manner alone was most disturbing. Mounting a rocket assembly on a parked car, aiming them at the office where he worked, and firing the entire barrage by remote control at the moment he sat down to his desk—all pointed to either an incredible coincidence, or a far more efficient intelligence network than, for example, that dossier on your desk would indicate. Furthermore, that same evening, as a precaution, without informing anyone, using a different passport, I fly to Lisbon. . . ."

". . . And time flies on apace," The Interrogator said. "You want, in short, to know how we did it?"

George nodded.

The Interrogator nodded back, then rummaged through a lower drawer, coming up with a small reel of recording tape. He gave George a speculative look, said: "I don't see what harm it can do at this late hour," slipped the reel onto the recorder beside his desk, and began guiding the ribbon around the spools.

George did not recognize the first voice, a man's which said only: "September 18th; 6:15 A.M., New York time." Following this he heard an unknown woman ask two questions in scarcely audible French. The next speaker, however, he placed at once:

"Oui. Oui. Hello, George. How gauche of you to call collect."

"Our friends are most upset about the Colonel's unfortunate demise, Abdul."

"It was unavoidable, George. Ask any actuary: indecisiveness and a tendency to gamble recklessly make for a poor driving risk. Quite frankly, I no longer trusted him behind the wheel."

"They wish you had informed them of his condition beforehand. They feel the accident might have been averted had you followed customary procedure."

"There wasn't time, George. The man was dangerous. . . ."

George stared with rapt dumb fascination at the Interrogator.

Who was amused. Whose smile at last bore traces of genuine warmth. Who switched off the recorder and said: "Surprise, surprise."

# Five

~~

*Baker*: I think a brief review would be in order at this juncture. Now, from 5:17 to 5:34—in other words, between the time those bombs went off and that point at which the water submerged the catwalk, the details to bear in mind are (*as before, ticking off each fact with a fingertip*): the traffic jams on both sides of the river; the north and center tubes impassable except by foot; one patrolman left at the Manhattan exit (those two detectives having been knocked unconscious when the Land Rover exploded); two officers from the Dairy Queen on duty at the Jersey portal; the sand barges sent for; police units on their way; a handful of people still alive in the water; and that bearded terrorist on the Jersey catwalk. (*Raises his hand*) Any questions?

*Goldwater* (*who has not been listening*): Is it true, Mr. Sultan, that the lower wind chamber was almost empty at the time the catwalk flooded?

*Sultan*: Not exactly. It was one-third full by my calculations.

*Goldwater*: I find that difficult to understand.

*Sultan*: Well, to put it in the simplest terms possible: the amount coming in exceeded the amount that could be siphoned off through the air ducts along the curbing—which are not much bigger than street gutters. Actually, of course, it is far more complicated than that. But I won't burden you with a lecture on hydraulics. The fact

~~

is: X number of gallons had to accumulate in the tube before a steady rate of drainage could develop.

*Goldwater* (*tentatively*): You mean, the water had to slow down?

*Sultan* (*nods*): And thereby acquire hydrostatic equilibrium. Unfortunately, this didn't happen until the level was six inches from the catwalk.

*Javits*: How long did it take to fill the chamber, Mr. Sultan?

*Sultan*: Approximately 30 minutes. It was full by 5:45.

*Javits*: And how deep was the water in the roadway by then?

*Sultan*: Five feet. Most of the cars had been swamped.

*Baker*: And we are getting ahead of ourselves again. Let's talk about the mudslide at the New York end. Which occurred (*searches for the entry in his notes, frowns, looks up*) . . . when, Mr. Sultan?

*Sultan*: At 5:37—less than a minute after the Land Rover exploded.

*Baker*: Can you explain why it caved in, without becoming unduly technical?

*Sultan*: You have to picture that hole in the riverbed . . .

\*

. . . which was like a well 16 feet deep that from the start had been emptying sand and silt in suspension along with boulders that bombarded the roof until the hole had enlarged to twice its original size; just as the well itself expanded—growing concentrically wider and wider as suction scooped out the sides until the western wall simply gave way and sank in one long plunge that tore out 10 more feet of roof and funneled 130 tons of muck into the tube at such an angle that it built up a ceiling-high dune 35 feet long that clogged the roadway almost to the ramp before a huge slab of shale broke loose from the riverbed and closed the hole. . . .

*Jackson*: Stopped it up? The tunnel? Completely?

*Sultan*: Like a cork in a bottle.

*Goldwater*: What about the overhead wind chamber, Mr. Sultan?

*Sultan*: We tried that. It was plugged solid, too.

*Moynihan (sitting upright with a sudden idea)*: You waited half an hour to test the overhead route, Mr. Sultan?

*Sultan*: No, as a matter of fact. I shut off the fans and sent a man at each portal topside around 5:20. But there was a solid wall of water across both ends of the chamber. And no one, Mr. Moynihan, could have walked through a nine-ton head of water. Clark Kent works for the *Daily Planet*, not the Port Authority.

*Moynihan (leaning forward to zero in)*: But those two bomb holes were located over the roadway, 50 feet beyond each ramp. Your men could have opened fire on the terrorists from nearby air vents without having to brave the water. And what a pity you allowed such an opportunity to slip by, Mr. Sultan. *(Bitterly)* Had you been thinking, the disaster might well have been averted.

*Sultan (shakes his head in disgust)*: There was a layer of silt a foot thick in the chamber, for your information. And six inches of running water covering that. Oozing constantly through the vents like rain. So in order to carry on a fight from the ceiling, we would have had to unbolt the louvers, which would have taken ten minutes had the walkway been dry. And even with the louvers off, my men would have had to shoot through a film of water. But more importantly, as I'm sure you can appreciate by now, we were somewhat pressed for time.

*Baker (hastily)*: As is this committee, gentlemen. Let us, therefore, pick up where we left off with that bearded assassin over in Jersey, Mr. Sultan.

*Sultan*: He jumped off the catwalk and went down near the bottom of the ramp to retrieve that box of grenades, dragging it up to the Pettibone—which had stopped in more or less the same spot where the Cadillac had been. This was about 5:30.

*Moynihan (holding up a sheet of paper as if exhibiting it in court)*: There must be some mistake in this report, Mr. Sultan. It says here that your men made no further attempt to rush the terrorist.

*Sultan*: That's right.

*Moynihan*: Then I am truly confused. I thought the order of the day was to rescue those people trapped inside.

*Sultan*: With what? Our bare hands? I had two fifty-year-old desk jockeys from the Dairy Queen at my disposal. There were strong young men drowning in there, you know. How long do you suppose a couple of aging, pot-bellied control panelists would have lasted? Providing, that is, they could have made it past the killer, who cancelled that possibility by lobbing a grenade around the curve every thirty seconds until the catwalk went under water. We couldn't even risk going in to put out the fires until 5:35. And besides, to tell you the truth, I was sick of sending people to their death, especially when the sacrifice would have served no useful purpose whatsoever.

*Moynihan*: Have you had much experience playing God, Mr. Sultan?

*Sultan*: No—but then I am not a politician.

*Baker*: And I refuse to act as devil's advocate for either one of you any longer. This is a Federal investigation, not the backdrop for your private debate, so I suggest we get *on* with the business at hand. (*Pauses to compose himself*) Now—I understand, Mr. Sultan, that the terrorist committed suicide to avoid being captured. Would you elaborate on that for us?

*Sultan*: At 5:50 the first outside reinforcements reached the Jersey side—a four-man squad from the New Jersey State Police who landed outside the portals in a helicopter. I outlined the situation to them over the intercom, and they went into action five minutes later, armed with heavy automatic rifles and bullet-proof vests. The terrorist wounded two of them with a grenade, taking a bullet through the chest in the process. He fell down behind the snowplow, didn't move while the troopers dragged their injured out. After a bit, though, he pulled himself into a sitting position against the blade. He was losing a lot of blood, kept dropping his head like a drunk, so we decided to give it another minute. Thirty seconds later, at 5:56, he picked up a grenade, pulled the pin, and dropped it back into the box. The explosion twisted the blade into a vertical position.

*Stennis* (*abruptly*): Whatever happened to the patrolman on the roof of that catwalk booth, Mr. Sultan?

*Sultan* (*reluctantly*): He had been watching the camera across from him for a long time. Sat there with his legs hanging down, almost touching the water. Crying, staring at the bodies. He stood up when that bearded terrorist detonated the box of grenades. At 5:58 he waved goodbye to the camera and jumped. The current carried him under fast.

*Abzug*: This would be about the time the girl in that floating Honda appeared, Mr. Sultan?

*Sultan*: Yes. One of the computer technicians spotted her just before six o'clock.

*Abzug* (*appealing to the table*): Will someone please tell me how a car could have remained afloat in there?

*Goldwater*: It isn't all that farfetched, really. They make those little cars airtight. Last summer, in fact, the Coast Guard found a Volkswagen floating three miles out to sea off San Diego, riding high and dry. A young couple had parked it in a ravine near the shore. They went up into the rocks to . . . and, anyway, it was dark when they returned—only to discover that the tide had swept into the ravine, carrying their car away. . . .

*Baker* (*studying his wristwatch*): I see no need to dwell at length on the mystery of the sea-going Honda. The fact remains that it floated, although I'm sure only God and the Japanese know why. Having lost consciousness from a blow on the head, the young lady came to just before her car began its unorthodox maiden voyage. You take it from there, Mr. Sultan.

*Sultan*: No one had been paying much attention to the Honda. We assumed it was empty. It was sticking out sideways from the south wall, anchored by the front bumper to a stack of cars about 400 yards east of the Jersey ramp—the girl in the driver's seat, scared out of her wits, staring wide-eyed around her. She screamed when the bumper snapped free, her mouth forming a big O as the

Honda launched itself into the current backwards. It struck a submerged car and rotated, then started navigating headfirst toward New York.

*Goldwater*: How deep was the water now, Mr. Sultan?

*Sultan*: Seven feet and rising.

*Goldwater*: Still violent?

*Sultan*: Well—yes and no.

*Baker*: I'll have to ask you to decipher that, Mr. Sultan.

*Sultan*: The current ran strong for 200 yards, until it crashed into a chain of cars protruding across the roadway like a barrier reef. After breaking over the wreckage, the flow dissipated—slowing down gradually during the next 1300 yards before it rippled against that trailer near the New York end at a speed of about one knot. I do not mean to imply, however, that the Honda floated leisurely along. It twirled like a baton now and then, even went sideways once for a hundred yards. But it was remarkably buoyant—drawing water only to the fender wells; so it actually scraped over, rather than bumped into, the buried cars.

*Baker*: Could you give us a thumbnail sketch of the scene around that semi-cab and trailer, Mr. Sultan?

*Sultan*: The cab was still facing Manhattan, jacked in the air above the left lane, waves periodically washing across the frame. The trailer stood beside it almost at a right angle—serving as a breakwater but also deflecting the current into the north wall and producing a returning eddy in which clusters of bodies turned round and round in a wide, foaming orbit. On the other side of the trailer, to the right of the cab, a mound of cars rose several feet above the water with that pickup still on top—sitting broadside: the front end facing the camera, the bed sloping down.

*Jackson*: Were there any journalists on hand, Mr. Sultan?

*Sultan*: The place was beginning to crawl with them. Before it was over, they outnumbered the police two to one. They arrived in helicopters with emergency medical teams disguised as doctors. They came in ambulances, on foot, they rented boats—I wouldn't be surprised if some of them had swum the river. They stood on cars, on each other's shoulders; hung by their toes from the overpasses taking pictures every time the police brought out a body.

*Baker*: And on that gruesome note, let us rejoin the young lady and her Honda.

*Sultan*: By 6:05 she had traveled 500 yards without serious incident, which led me to conclude that, unless it sank, the Honda would presently dock at the semi, and that if we could reach that ruptured air vent above the cab, we had a chance to save the girl.

*Stennis*: Hold it, Mr. Sultan. I thought you said that wind chamber was plugged with sand.

*Sultan*: It was. Twenty-eight feet of it, that is. But I still had the fans.

*Stennis* (*mulls this over briefly*): How big *is* that chamber?

*Sultan*: Four feet, six inches high, and fifteen feet across.

*Stennis* (*more mulling*): That works out to a *powerful* lot of sand, Mr. Sultan. Wet sand, to boot.

*Sultan*: True. But there are two ventilation towers on the New York side, and the sand lay between them. Both turbine systems generate enormous suction winds. Wide open, they can build to speeds in excess of ninety miles an hour.

*Javits*: Mr. Sultan, you say that this idea came to you at 6:05. Yet according to the FBI report, you didn't activate the fans until 6:11. Why the delay?

*Sultan*: I was afraid the sand would choke the sorting assemblies and burn up the generators, dousing every light in the tube for three minutes until we could transfer to emergency power.

*Javits*: Three minutes? Isn't that procedure handled by computers?

*Sultan*: Normally, yes. But those particular computers respond to sensors under the roadway, and the system was malfunctioning due to the weight of the water. So I didn't want to gamble on a manual transfer to emergency power and a three-minute blackout until they had reached the semi.

*Jackson*: They?

*Sultan*: Yes. She was no longer by herself.

*Baker*: And we have outdistanced ourselves once more. Time now, Mr. Sultan, to drop back to 6:05—the Honda bobbing without incident, the girl as yet alone.

*Sultan*: Within two minutes her front bumper snagged on a string of cars projecting from the north wall like a pier. There were several victims caught in the metal above the water line—two women, a little boy, a man lying on a hood. At 6:09 the man suddenly sat up. He made some sort of hand-signals to the girl, then rocked the bumper loose and grabbed the side mirror as the Honda nosed into the open.

I turned on the fans as they floated through those bodies coiling at the New York end, the man paddling with one arm to offset the eddy. The Honda thumped into the trailer and then drifted with the eddy to the cab, where the main current reasserted itself: pinning the car lengthwise against the rear of the frame. The man hoisted himself onto the frame and stood up beside that big round trailer hitch. He was gesturing to the girl, pointing to the ceiling. She rolled down the window and shinnied into his arms. And then they started up, climbing slowly, hampered by waves swelling over the undercarriage and spray flying in their faces. It took them nearly three minutes to reach the cab and crawl across its flattened top to the hood.

*Javits*: And by now, of course, you had recognized him.

*Sultan*: Yes.

*Javits*: Because of the eyepatch?

*Sultan*: That. But I could also make out his face, and the fact that he had a bad head wound. It was the General, all right.

*Baker*: When did you shut down the fans, Mr. Sultan?

*Sultan*: While they were crawling over the cab. The winds had cleared away all but ten inches of sand. Three Manhattan policemen started into the chamber at 6:14—at almost the exact instant that the General boosted the girl through the vent.

*Moynihan*: How was it, Mr. Sultan, that not one of those policemen reached the air vent?

*Sultan*: You'll recall that the mudslide had torn out most of the roof when it slammed through the bomb hole, which was now a crater—wave action having long since eroded the material directly beneath. All that remained of the roof was a 30-inch ledge along the south side. One policeman went across alone, to make certain that the rafters would support his weight. The girl was waiting for him on the other side. Meanwhile, the sand around that piece of shale was beginning to shake loose. Fearing another slide, and expecting the General to show up at any moment, he led the girl across to safety.

*Abzug*: What happened to the General?

*Sultan*: That killer from the New York end happened. He pulled himself off the bed of that pickup shortly after the girl disappeared into the chamber.

*Baker*: You are quite certain it was the same man?

*Sultan*: Positive. He still had the turban knotted around his head. He was waving his arms, calling for help. I think his legs were broken. And he appeared to be blind: kept turning his head, looking nearly straight up, hanging there on his elbows.

*Abzug*: What did the General do?

*Sultan*: He was climbing into the chamber when the terrorist started shouting. He froze, then dropped back onto the hood and turned. He cupped his hands and shouted. And then he came down from the cab to help the killer. But it was too late. Because at 6:15, right on schedule, as the General took the other man's hand, those two barges released their load. The impact shook loose another 30 tons of sand into the roadway, creating a ceiling-high wave that churned westward for 500 yards. After the camera lens cleared, the pickup was gone and so were they. We didn't recover their bodies until the next morning.

*Baker* (*looking at his watch again*): I think that will be all for today, Mr. Sultan.

# Six

~

"Strictly as one professional to another," said the Interrogator, "let me congratulate you: Boule's death was a remarkably clever stroke. We at first assumed it was the prelude to some sort of an attempt on Rothschild. Luckily, our people turned up those killers before the ubiquitous Rousseau could sniff them out. You must have paid that ringleader handsomely. A more stupid, obstinate man I have never met. We have extracted more information from mutes. Before dying, however, he did mention a telephone number."

George cursed.

"Most careless of you, I agree. Not that your presence in the plot shed any real new light. Our files described you as a harmless financial contributor to the cause. Nonetheless, to be on the safe side, we placed you under surveillance. At the same time, it being expedient to muzzle Rousseau, we asked the Baron to use his influence in persuading the Parisians to close the case on Boule. An uneventful week went by. Then Straus bought his mother a new Citroen."

George cursed again.

"An understandable oversight on your part," the Interrogator said graciously, "as he went through a dealer in Grenoble. Which, if anything, left us further in the dark: for this sudden increase in

171

his standard of living only cemented our conviction that your group was planning to snatch Rothschild and hold him for ransom.

George was beginning to see it. "You followed me to New York."

"And from thence to the Algonquin and Abdul. Who of course was a complete unknown. So we put a tail on him. Likewise on your nefarious Colonel. We even assigned an agent to monitor the coital activities of that Dutch whore and the late Martin Rugg. All of which led us increasingly nowhere. After two weeks in New York, we had come up with nothing that made the slightest hole in our kidnapping hypothesis."

"Not even the boat?"

The Interrogator smiled ruefully. "On the contrary; we thought you intended holding the Baron incognito on the *Vita-Vita* until the ransom was paid."

"And then Ali and the others entered the picture."

"Precisely. Ali may have been a stranger, but our records on his companions constituted a veritable rogue's gallery. It was intriguing, actually: four well-known terrorists, all demolition experts, each a veteran scuba diver, suddenly converging on Manhattan— to what end, we had no inkling. The whole business had taken on a new and quite fascinating dimension. So we waited, watched, rented a boat, filmed one of your friends placing that charge under the Colonel's car, hired a helicopter and filmed several dozen of those curious expeditions to and from Newark Airport. As early on as mid-September it was obvious that the *mise-en-scène* was to be the Lincoln Tunnel. Adding Rothschild to the script provided us the clue to your intended victim."

"You let it happen," George said uncertainly.

"We did nothing to stop it," the Interrogator temporized.

George seemed to be in pain. "But why?"

"Self-preservation," the Interrogator explained. "The General was never our choice, you must know. The Americans, largely on the basis of his legendary influence with the Pentagon, shoved him down our throat."

"And he in turn made you swallow the prime ministership."

"Along with one additional and extremely bitter pill. He forced us to agree—in writing, no less—that once our nuclear capability was complete, we would announce the fact publicly and begin immediate formal proceedings to establish a Palestinian state."

George absorbed this slowly, looking like man just informed of his wife's infidelity.

"Which was absolute madness," the Interrogator said huffily. "You did us a favor, really. We would have been obliged to eliminate him on our own, sooner or later. Now instead, without lifting a finger, we have been delivered of a menace and granted a martyr in one fell swoop. Not to mention the added bonus of an international anti-Palestinian campaign that promises to be of some duration, and of course the plutonium. Indeed, things could not have worked out more to our advantage had we planned it ourselves."

George fumbled for words: "Then . . . what happened in the tunnel . . ."

". . . A minor production," the Interrogator said. "The main event took place offstage."

And George finally saw most of it. "That's why you left me on the string. Your men could have snuffed me at any time, but they were waiting for me to lead them to the Committee. Because like Ali and Straus, they all have to go, don't they? With them out of the way, you and your friend in the Oval Office can keep that embarrassing nuclear pact a secret and chalk the whole affair off as just another senseless Arab atrocity." He spat on the desk. "You are worse than we are."

"One other thing," the Interrogator said quietly.

And George suddenly saw everything.

As the Interrogator added: "—There are no Americans coming for you," and thumbed the voltage regulator.

# Coda

~~

Months later, in that section of their final report entitled *Rumors*, the Commission made it official:

*4. Item: On October 19, the Palestinian news agency WAFA issued a release stating that the underlying motive behind the General's visit to this country was to conclude negotiations pursuant to a clandestine nuclear treaty between Israel and the United States.*

Comment: No such treaty, clandestine or otherwise, exists.

It was that simple.

~~

Cunningham, Richard,
1939-

A ceremony in the
Lincoln Tunnel

| DATE | | | |
|---|---|---|---|
| | | | |
| | | | |
| | | | |
| | | | |
| | | | |
| | | | |
| | | | |
| | | | |
| | | | |
| | | | |
| | | | |